OSWAIN AND THE GUILD OF THE WHITE EAGLE

For Andrew

Oswain
and the
Guild of the
White Eagle

JOHN HOUGHTON

KINGSWAY PUBLICATIONS
EASTBOURNE

First published as *Feldrog's Sting* in 1993
This substantially revised edition 2003

ISBN 0 85476 971 4

Published by
KINGSWAY COMMUNICATIONS LTD
Lottbridge Drove, Eastbourne BN23 6NT, England.
Email: books@kingsway.co.uk

Book design and production for the publishers by
Bookprint Creative Services, P.O. Box 827, BN21 3YJ, England.
Printed in Great Britain.

Contents

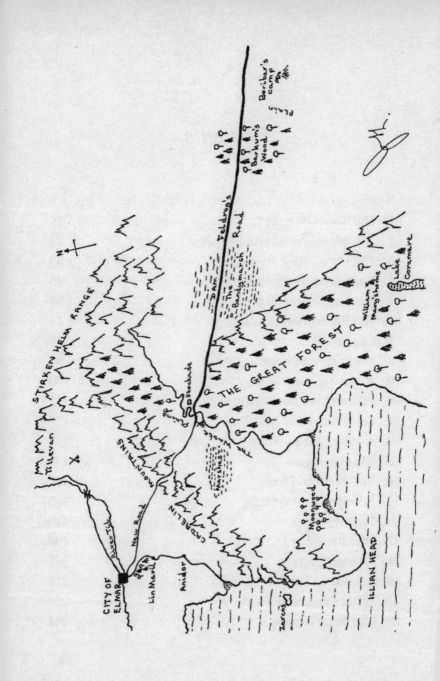

Prologue

Oswain groaned in his sleep. The pale face of the Ice Maiden flickered on the screen of his fevered mind. Loriana was calling for him, and her voice was full of anxiety. He tried to answer, but her face faded and in its place appeared a splendid jewel that glinted and flashed like a single brilliant star in the night. He winced. The light pulsed in perfect time with the throbbing pain in his leg.

For a while he tossed and turned on his crude bed of straw, but sleep had deserted him. He woke and lay on his back in silence, staring blankly into the darkness of his cell. How long had it been, he wondered? Six days? Six months or six years? What did it matter? He was a helpless prisoner, far from home, and his left leg was broken in two places.

The wooden door of his prison crashed open. Oswain flinched at the sudden light. The sunshine made him long for the open skies and the rich colours of his home in the Great Forest of Alamore. He had friends and loved ones waiting there, no doubt hoping for his safe return. The Merestone, the fabled jewel that shimmered across the Enchanted Glade and made the forest so special, was calling him home, and urgently. But he was trapped.

Atag's bulky form filled the doorway. He laughed, coarse and cruel, at Oswain's plight. Then, with a sneer of contempt, he set a mug of water and a hunk of stale bread on the floor. Oswain would have to drag his body painfully across the rough wooden planks to reach this miserable fare. But he expected no better. The word 'pity' had no meaning for Boribars like Atag.

The door slammed shut and with its closing died Oswain's hopes for yet another day.

* * *

Far away in an altogether different world, Peter Brown woke with a start. The piercing shriek of an eagle echoed in his brain. He glanced across to where his brother slept.

'Are you awake, Andrew?' he hissed.

'You heard it too then?' Andrew replied sleepily. 'I thought I was just dreaming.'

'That was no dream,' Peter answered gravely. 'That was Arca's call. We're needed back in the Great Forest, and I reckon it's urgent! We'd better tell Sarah.'

'I bet she already knows,' Andrew yawned. 'She always does. Leave it till morning.' He sighed. 'Mum and Dad will only tell us off if we. . . . '

Andrew drifted back to sleep. But Peter lay awake for a long time, wondering what it all meant and when their adventure would start.

*   *   *

Duron the Hunter strung his bow and checked his arrows.

His stern face betrayed no emotion and his steely eyes were cold as ice. So long as they paid him well for the job, he did not concern himself with the ambitions of those he served. Feldrog had hired the best, and was generous with his gold. That was good enough. Duron had his instructions and he would ensure full satisfaction for his new master.

1

The Secret Tunnel

Sarah gazed wistfully through the latticed window of her bedroom.

It was late September and she was staying with her parents and her brothers in a little Sussex cottage called Homemead. It was on the edge of the Pevensey marshes and they had rented it for the weekend as a special treat.

A pale golden mist lay across the damp fields and the early morning sun hung low on the horizon, a disc of crimson fire that flashed burnished highlights on Sarah's blonde hair and kissed her honeyed skin with a blush of rose. Still warm from her slumbers, she opened the casement, smiled her serene smile and breathed the cool air. It was sharp with the tang of early autumn, chilled cranberry sorbet all covered in wine. Rich russet leaves lay in curled flurries beneath the windless trees and spiders' webs heavy with sparkling dew hung like tiaras on the dark brambles. Somewhere across the marshes a flock of Canada geese rose in the dawn. Their faint mournful cry carried over the mists and Sarah was filled with a soft sadness for the memories of summers past. She sighed deeply.

Just recently they had received the news that Uncle Joe's old oak had blown down in a fierce storm that had swept across the south of England. The tree was special because she and her two brothers had once entered Oswain's enchanted realm, Caris Meriac, through a mysterious stairway in its trunk. Although there were many other ways into the Land Beyond the Far Places, as it was sometimes known, with the oak's destruction Sarah felt as if a family pet had died. She could feel the tears in her eyes as she thought about it. Suddenly she longed with all her heart to be back in the Great Forest of Alamore with Oswain and Trotter and all her other friends.

Her thoughts were abruptly broken by the door flying open as her two brothers came barging into the room.

'Hi, Sarah! You awake then?' cried Andrew.

'What do you think?' she answered shortly, irritated by this rude interruption to her thoughts.

Andrew, cheerful as ever and not put off in the slightest by her manner, gazed quizzically at his sister with his head to one side.

'You know, I'm not really sure, Pete,' he said to his brother. 'Maybe she's just sleepwalking.'

'And sleep-talking too!' Peter added with a grin.

Sarah grabbed a pillow and threw it in their direction. It missed.

'OK, you two. What do you want?' she demanded.

The boys bounced onto her bed, suddenly serious.

'Arca,' said Peter tersely. 'Did you hear him last night? Because we did. Both of us.'

Sarah's mood changed at once. Arca was the great white eagle, the servant of Elmesh, who had played an important part in their previous adventures in Oswain's world. She wanted to know exactly what they had heard. As they told her, she understood why she was feeling the way she was.

'I was just thinking about Oswain and everybody when you came in,' she explained. 'It made me feel that I really want to go back there again. And this time for ever,' she added intensely.

'I told Peter you would hear the call differently from us,' Andrew piped up. 'I said you would know, 'cos it would be just like you to have a dream . . . or a feeling, wouldn't it?'

Sarah nodded thoughtfully.

'I feel we've got to get there as soon as possible,' she said earnestly. 'The question is, how? I mean we can't just wish it, can we?'

'But we can't force our way in either,' Peter answered sensibly. 'The problem is, it has always happened so unexpectedly in the past. This time it's different because we've been . . . well . . . sort of forewarned. All we can do is wait, I suppose,' he ended lamely.

A call from their mother to come down and have breakfast ended their discussions for the time being.

* * *

After breakfast and washing and dressing in jeans and sweatshirts, the three children set out on a walk across the marshes. They figured that it was no use just sitting around all day waiting for something to happen. In any case, it was a splendid morning. The sun had quickly burned away the early mist and now shone warmly on the trees and hedges and fields which simply beckoned to be enjoyed.

Peter Brown at thirteen was the eldest. His new form tutor was Miss Sturron, a pleasant enough teacher, but who in his mind quickly became known as The Mysteron, not least because she had replaced Mr Pyle and nobody knew what had become of him, and the most obvious explanation, apart from the boringly sensible fact that he might have changed schools, was that he had been taken over by an alien!

Sarah, aged eleven, was quietly hating her new school. All the other girls seemed bitchy and cliquey and all the lessons were boring. The fact that she was becoming more than a little snooty herself escaped her notice; her mother just called it growing up.

Andrew at ten was one of the eldest in his year and was feeling top of the tree. He had also taken to playing the drums and the walls of his upstairs bedroom regularly shook, much to the annoyance of everyone else.

All in all, a weekend away just after the start of a new school year seemed a great idea – though Andrew had been forbidden to bring his drums; something about disturbing the peace of the countryside, his father had said.

They took a path across the marshes towards the little market town of Hailsham. It led alongside a deep dyke

– one of the many that criss-crossed the marsh and kept it drained. Before long they had put their earlier thoughts to the back of their minds as the sights and sounds of the countryside absorbed their interest. Peter spotted Canada geese and a moorhen. They even came across a solitary heron brooding by the water's edge. While Peter sat watching it, Andrew and Sarah discovered some brambles in a nearby hedge. They were soon busy picking blackberries.

Suddenly, Andrew gave a yell. 'Here, you two! Come and have a look at this! I think I've just found a badger's sett.'

Intrigued, Peter and Sarah joined him to take a look. He showed them a small opening half-covered with brambles at the base of the hedgerow.

'I don't think it's a sett,' said Peter. 'There's no sign of any spoor and. . . .' He paused as gingerly he pulled back the brambles to reveal a hole of about half a metre across. 'Hey, wait a minute . . . take look at this . . . it's made of bricks,' he exclaimed. 'It must be some old building remains. Let's have a look inside.'

Ignoring Sarah's warning to be careful, Peter poked his head into the hole.

'It's very dark and I can't see very much,' his voice boomed. 'But it's not a cellar or anything like that. I think it's some kind of tunnel. Anyway, it's almost large enough to stand up in, I reckon. Pity we haven't got torches, or we could explore it.'

'Hey, I read about a tunnel around here,' exclaimed Andrew. 'It was in one of Dad's local guidebooks.

Boring stuff mostly, but it said that years ago there was a tunnel used for hiding priests when their enemies were hunting for them. The trouble is, nobody knows where it is any more.'

'Perhaps we've found it, then,' said Peter, full of enthusiasm. He withdrew his head from the hole. 'We could become famous and have our pictures in the newspapers.'

'I thought it was me who discovered it first,' retorted Andrew. 'Still, you can both be in the pictures as my assistants,' he added with good nature. 'I tell you what, why don't we go back and get our torches and then we can explore it properly?'

'Tunnels are dangerous. You never know when they are going to collapse,' Sarah warned half-heartedly, but she shut up as soon as she saw the looks on her brothers' faces.

An hour later the children returned with their torches to the opening in the bank, squeezed through it and dropped into the tunnel. No one said as much, but each of them was thinking that this was perhaps the way they would get back into the Great Forest. That possibility made them forget everything else they should have thought about, including telling their parents where they were going.

Once inside, they discovered that the tunnel was brick-built and about one and a half metres in diameter. Apart from a small trickle of water on the floor, it was quite dry.

'Which way shall we go?' asked Peter. His voice

sounded hollow in the enclosed space.

'Well, not that way, that's for sure,' said Andrew flashing his torch to the left. 'Look. It's blocked solid.'

Sure enough, they could see that the tunnel had caved in just a short way along from where they were crouching.

'Well that settles it, then,' said Peter brightly. 'We'll go the other way.'

So, with the beams from their torches reflecting off the lime-encrusted brickwork, the three children set off into the gloom. They had to stoop to avoid banging their heads on the roof as they went.

'I wonder if this will lead us straight into the Great Forest,' said Sarah, at last giving voice to all their thoughts.

'Perhaps we'll come out straight into Trotter's house. Imagine his surprise when he sees us!' Andrew cried.

Imagine then the children's disappointment when, three minutes later, they came upon another roof fall. It totally barred their path.

'No, it's no use,' said Peter with a shrug, after he had clambered around the fallen brickwork. 'We'll just have to go back, that's all.'

Glumly, his brother and sister agreed and they began to retrace their steps.

'Bit of a silly idea, anyway, I suppose,' said Andrew. They reached the entrance and clambered out into the open air.

Sarah sighed deeply. She was close to tears. 'But Oswain needs us,' she exclaimed. 'There must be a way in somewhere. But where is it?'

At that moment there was a loud splash from the dyke. Peter stepped to the edge of the steep bank to see what it was. 'Oh, it's only the heron,' he said with mild disappointment. 'It's caught a fish.' He paused. 'Hey, it's a whopper, though. Come and have a look.'

Sarah and Andrew, not greatly interested, joined him on the edge.

What happened next took all three by surprise.

Possibly the edge of the dyke was muddy or crumbly. Maybe Peter was concentrating too much on the heron. Perhaps their disappointment over not reaching the Great Forest had distracted them. Whatever the reason, Peter suddenly and unexpectedly lost his balance and he teetered uncontrollably on the edge of the bank. In a desperate effort to save himself, he grabbed for his brother. It all happened so quickly. With a cry of alarm, Andrew slipped on the grass and before they could stop themselves, both boys toppled head-over-heels down the bank towards the water. The heron took off in noisy fright.

But Peter and Andrew never hit the water.

It was impossible to say whether they slipped through a hidden duct in the bank, or whether something more mysterious happened. All Peter and Andrew knew as they fell was that suddenly everything had gone very dark. For a while each of them felt as though they were tumbling and floating through an empty space. It was like a very weird dream.

It ended as suddenly as it had begun. With a loud

squelch both boys came to rest in a tangled heap to find themselves splattered in mud and surrounded by tall reeds growing in shallow water. They were soaked to the skin.

'W-what happened?' gasped Andrew in a dazed voice.

'Glubble-thunk,' croaked a voice in response.

Peter and Andrew sat up with a start at the strange sound.

A furry duck-like creature confronted them. Brown mud covered it from top to tail and it gazed at them curiously through bright beady eyes.

'Glubble-thunk!' repeated the strange animal.

Andrew and Peter stared at one another in blank amazement.

'Where on earth are we?' gasped Peter.

* * *

Sarah, meanwhile, gazed dumbly down the bank where her brothers had fallen. They appeared simply to have vanished into thin air. For an awful moment she thought they must have drowned, but she had heard no splash, and in any case they were both good swimmers.

'Peter? Andrew? Are you all right?' she called anxiously.

There was no reply.

Carefully, she climbed down the bank to the water's

edge, but try as she might she could find no trace of their whereabouts. In a daze she clambered back to the path. What should she do? Should she run for help? Or had they managed somehow to enter Oswain's realm without her? Feeling very confused and unsure she sat back on her heels and pondered what to do next.

She was just on the point of deciding to take another look down the bank when she heard a faint scraping sound. The noise startled her and she leapt nervously to her feet, expecting to find someone standing behind her – and ready to half-kill Peter and Andrew if they were playing a joke on her!

To her relief there was nobody about, but the scraping noise continued.

Only then did Sarah realise that the noise was coming from the hole in the hedgerow. Filled with intrigue and some trepidation, she hurried across to the opening. Perhaps her brothers had somehow found another way into the tunnel from the water's edge.

'Peter? Are you there, Andrew?' she called anxiously.

Silence greeted her. The scraping had stopped.

Sarah made up her mind. Scared, but determined to solve the mystery, she climbed back into the tunnel.

Once she was inside, she saw to her surprise a shaft of light coming from the rock fall on the left. Filled with curiosity, she edged cautiously towards it and began to clamber across the jumbled bricks. A dazed feeling came over her as the light grew brighter and brighter. Then, all at once, she saw the end of the tunnel. She made her way towards it.

Moments later, feeling quite confused, Sarah emerged once more into broad daylight. However, instead of open marshland, she found herself surrounded by tall trees.

At once, it dawned on her. She had found the way into the Great Forest of Alamore! The sweetness of the air and the tingling sense of life left her in no doubt whatsoever. Sarah looked around her and gave a whoop of delight. This was the world where she *belonged* – not like boring old school and silly, bitchy girls!

She had emerged onto a surprisingly well-kept path, smooth and neatly edged. 'Very unusual for the Great Forest,' she thought. Someone must have been busy.

Sarah figured that she would eventually come across somebody she knew, whichever direction she took. So she decided to turn left and started walking.

The path ran very straight, and appeared to be completely deserted. After ten minutes of steady walking Sarah had still not met anybody. She was just wondering whether to cut off the track and into the undergrowth when she saw a bend ahead. Feeling hopeful, she quickened her pace, running the last few metres.

But what greeted her as she rounded the bend was so unexpected that it stopped Sarah dead in her tracks. She stared in open-mouthed amazement.

A bright red security barrier stretched right across the path. Next to it stood two very stern-looking hares armed with sharp-tipped spears. Clearly nobody would be able to pass further without their say-so.

Sarah approached the barrier slowly. The hares were suddenly alert and eyed her warily.

'Good day, stranger.' The one on the right stepped forward and spoke in an official tone of voice. 'Your pass, if you please. You cannot go beyond this checkpoint without showing it.'

2

Trouble in Wood and Marsh

Sarah could hardly believe her ears. Was this really the Great Forest that she knew and loved? There had never been any barriers like this before. Under Oswain's reign everyone had always enjoyed the greatest possible freedom. It was all very strange and Sarah began to wonder just what mischief was afoot. It also crossed her mind that this might not be the Great Forest after all.

'Um, I'm afraid I don't have one,' she stammered. 'I'm a visitor here. But I. . . .'

Sarah hesitated. Somehow the hare did not seem the sort to understand that she and her two brothers were Oswain's special friends. It occurred to her, too, that she had no idea whether these hares were friends or foes.

'My name is Sarah,' she said instead. Then she asked, just to make sure, 'This is the Great Forest of Alamore, isn't it?'

'Well yes, of course it is,' the hare replied testily. He looked surprised at Sarah's question. 'Surely you know where you are? And you should know that you need a pass to travel on this path.'

'I'm afraid I don't know where I am. At least, not exactly,' she answered. 'And I don't know anything about passes. I've never needed one before.'

At that moment the other hare stepped forward. He pointed the tip of his spear at Sarah and viewed her with suspicion through narrowed eyes. His nostrils twitched.

'Just a minute, Banter,' he said to his fellow-guard. 'I don't trust this one. Look at her. She's a child of man, if I'm not very much mistaken. You know what that might mean?'

The hare named Banter gave a curt nod and addressed Sarah sternly. 'We have checkpoints along all the paths in this part of the forest. How did you get this far without a pass? Where have you come from?' He too pointed his spear menacingly at the girl.

Sarah wasn't afraid, but she was at a loss for words. How could she tell these two that she had simply walked along a tunnel from her own world into theirs?

Her hesitation was sufficient for the two suspicious guards.

'You're right, Biff,' said Banter to his cohort. 'She's not to be trusted.' Then turning to Sarah, he said bluntly, 'You are under arrest on suspicion of spying, or worse. You must appear before the local judges, who will decide what to do with you.'

Sarah looked around. Her first instinct was to run for it.

'Don't even think about it,' said Biff grimly, reading her thoughts. 'We can run faster than you, and we have orders to strike down anyone who tries to escape arrest.'

Suppressing her alarm and her desire to flee, Sarah decided there and then that being arrested might not be so bad after all. Indeed, was she not held in high regard in Alamore and had she not been dubbed Lady Sarah in the palace of Elmar? At least she would meet someone in real authority, and matters would soon be sorted out in a civilised manner, and she would discover the whereabouts of her old friends. She realised too that the hares were only doing their jobs. Obviously there were problems in the Great Forest serious enough to need guards, and this must be why Elmesh had brought her back here.

'All right,' she said brightly. 'Arrest me and take me to your leader!'

Banter escorted Sarah in silence along a fenced path leading off the main track. After about ten minutes' walking, they came into a small clearing where a thatched hut stood. Another hare was on guard outside. Banter muttered something in his ear and the hare disappeared inside the hut. A few moments later he put his head round the door and nodded.

'In there,' Banter commanded curtly.

The room had plain white walls and was bare except for a long table behind which sat three pompous-looking hares wearing black gowns.

They viewed her coldly.

'You have been brought to appear before the people's court. Your name, if you please?' demanded the one in the centre.

'Sarah. Sarah Brown,' she answered. 'Now listen. . . .'

The hare held up his paw to silence her. 'You apparently do not possess a pass, yet you have travelled deep into the Republic of Alamore. That is not easy for honest people. What is your business in the Great Forest? How did you manage to get through all the other checkpoints without being challenged?' he demanded.

'I have come by my own route to see Oswain and Loriana. They are friends of mine,' she replied plainly. Sarah felt that telling the truth was the best policy. 'You need to know that I am Lady Sarah and, actually, I think they will be very cross when they find out that you have arrested me and treated me like this.' She tossed her head.

To Sarah's satisfaction her words had the desired effect. The three hares turned to one another and conferred agitatedly for several minutes. 'That's given you something to think about,' she thought smugly.

The senior hare addressed her.

'It is not possible for anyone to see the king or his consort. They are away on business,' he said shortly.

Sarah's countenance dropped with dismay. 'When will they be back?' she asked.

'That is top secret information,' answered the hare. 'I cannot tell you.'

'Then can I see Lord Trotter instead?' Sarah asked.

The hare gave her a puzzled frown.

'It is possible, I suppose, but he lives a long way to the north of here. I should add that he is very old, and does not usually see visitors,' he replied. 'He is retired.'

Sarah was overjoyed to discover that the old badger was still alive.

'He'll want to see me. That's why I've come here,' she answered brightly.

One of the other judges leaned forward and looked

Sarah in the eye. 'So you say. But how do we know that you are telling the truth? These are dangerous times and too many folk have fancy tales to recite,' he said shrewdly. 'Where are you from? Why have you come to the South when anyone who knew Lord Trotter would go to the North? How did you get this far without a pass? How many barriers have you slipped round? Who else is with you?'

His questions made Sarah's head spin. 'This is crazy!' she exclaimed. 'Don't you know? I'm Sarah, Lady Sarah, and I expect my two brothers are around somewhere too. We . . . I've come from a far country. I just walked here and I only came across one barrier. Elmesh sent me. . . .'

The senior hare held up his hand.

'Do not use the name of Elmesh to defend your actions,' he said sternly. 'Whatever the truth of your story, you do not have a pass. That means you have travelled by illegal paths. We have to judge that fact. You will kindly wait outside.'

Sarah opened her mouth to protest, but it was no good. Banter ushered her outside.

After a few minutes they recalled her. Glumly, she listened to their pronouncement.

'We find you guilty of trespassing. Although you carry no obvious weapons and you do not appear dangerous, we can take no chances. You may proceed no further. Instead, you will be escorted from the Republic of Alamore immediately.'

'You mean to say I can't see Trotter?' Sarah exclaimed. 'Or . . . or anyone else?'

'That is correct,' the judge replied. He nodded to Banter. 'You will escort this person to the next barrier to the south and pass her over to another guard. He will take her on to the next, and so forth, until she is out of our domain.'

Banter nodded smartly.

'I advise you to co-operate,' said the judge to Sarah. 'Now, you are dismissed.'

Reluctantly Sarah agreed and, feeling very glum, she left the courtroom accompanied by Banter. This was not the adventure she had been hoping for. Perhaps Peter and Andrew were faring better. She wondered where they were. Maybe they were with Oswain and Loriana already. 'Lucky beggars! I bet they're having a great time!' she thought enviously.

* * *

Peter and Andrew were, in fact, trying to sort out their own predicament. They continued to stare in amazement at the strange creature that had greeted them.

'What on earth do you think it is?' Andrew asked Peter.

Peter looked at the animal carefully. It could have been a duck judging from its dun-coloured bill and its bright beady eyes. But he had never come across a brown furry duck that was completely smothered in mud and appeared to have no wings?

'I don't know,' said Peter. 'It looks like a talking mudpie. I think it's harmless, though. Do you think it understands us?'

'Let's find out,' Andrew proposed. 'Hello,' he said, addressing the creature. 'My name is Andrew and this is my brother, Peter. How do you do?'

'Glubble-thunk,' answered the creature. 'Glubble-thunk. Spliggle-bloth!'

'This is hopeless!' Andrew exclaimed.

'Blerp-glob-glob!' responded the odd creature.

The boys looked around them to see if they could obtain any clues to their predicament. They were sitting in only a few centimetres of water on what felt like very squelchy mud. The tall reeds that rose all around them hid everything else from sight, but overhead the sky was blue and the sun shone brightly.

'It seems that we're in a marsh of some kind,' said Peter – rather obviously, Andrew thought. 'I don't think it can be the Great Forest, because I can't remember anything like this, can you?'

Andrew shook his head and stood carefully to his feet. At once he had the uncomfortable feeling of his trainers filling up with mud. It wasn't worth the effort anyway, because he was not tall enough to see through the reeds. He crouched down again and shrugged his shoulders.

'Can't see a thing,' he said. 'And we're not going to get any sense out of him. So what do we do now?'

Suddenly there was a noisy rustling in the reeds. Peter and Andrew ducked down and waited anxiously in case it meant trouble. The next moment the reeds parted to reveal another creature of the same kind, only it was very much larger than the first.

'Oh, there you are, Glubble-thunk. I wondered where you had got to, running away from your mother like that! You're a naughty boy,' the creature squawked as it waded into view.

'Blerp!' replied Glubble-thunk.

Then his mother noticed Peter and Andrew crouching in the reeds.

'Good gracious me! You gave me quite a start. Goodness me! Who on marsh are you?' She waddled across and peered closely at them. 'Um, yes, who are you indeed?'

Peter and Andrew found her gaze a bit embarrassing but she seemed harmless enough. At least now they had someone they could understand. Perhaps they could find out just where they were and what was going on.

The creature cocked her head to one side and continued to examine them.

'Hm. So you must be the ones, by the looks of it. Stand up, both of you,' she said.

Somewhat sheepishly, the boys obeyed. 'Yes, indeed. Children of man and no mistake, from what I've been told. Well, good. And not before time too, I'm sure. You had better come at once and meet my husband and the others. Follow me, please. Oh, and you can call me Mrs Glub,' she added as an afterthought. 'Come on, Glubble-thunk.'

Peter and Andrew stared at one another with a mixture of incredulity and relief. Glubble-thunk was obviously still a baby and could only just about say his own name. But who were these strange creatures who were expecting them? And who told them the boys were coming? Agog to find out more they followed Mrs Glub and her wayward son through the marshes.

Splashing through the reeds the boys introduced themselves properly. They learned that they had landed in the middle of the Bandymarsh. It was home to a flock of flightless marsh-dwellers called Glumps.

'It's not far now,' explained Mrs Glub. 'My husband and the other drakes will explain everything to you. Although Elmesh only knows what you can do about it. I suppose I thought you would be very much bigger than you are. Still, I expect you are used to this sort of problem by now and you must know what you are doing otherwise Elmesh wouldn't have sent you, would he?'

Peter and Andrew glanced apprehensively at one another. They had heard this sort of thing before.

Suddenly there was a bright flash of light in the sky above. A loud boom followed instantly.

'Quick! Get down and cover your heads,' squawked Mrs Glub. She buried her son protectively somewhere in her muddy body.

The next instant, a great shower of rubble, mud and water poured out of the sky.

'Ouch, ouch!' cried Peter and Andrew in unison as they ducked and tried to protect themselves from the flying debris.

Another flash filled the sky, followed by an even louder bang. This time quite large pieces of rock fell all around them as they cowered in the reeds.

For a long time nobody moved. Then, when all seemed quiet, Mrs Glub let her son out from beneath her. He emerged with an indignant squawk.

'Whew, thank goodness that's over' exclaimed Peter. 'What was it all about? It sounded like an explosion.'

He turned to Andrew.

But to Peter's horror his brother was lying face down in the shallow water and next to him was a sizeable chunk of rock. A slight trickle of blood oozed from a large lump on the back of his head.

Hastily and full of alarm Peter yanked his brother from the water.

'Andrew, Andrew, are you all right? Say something!' he yelled.

But there was no reply from Andrew's pallid lips.

Peter gazed about him in panic. What was he going to do?

3

The Etins are Coming!

Andrew groaned aloud and then coughed.

Gingerly he felt his throbbing head and found a lump the size of an egg. All he could remember was the hail of falling rocks and then the sudden pain followed by darkness. With an effort he forced open his eyes. Close to his face was a familiar pink fuzzy shape. He closed his eyes and turned his head to one side. Slowly, he opened them again and gazed at his surroundings. Pale light filtered dimly through the walls of what looked like a room built of reeds. He seemed to be lying on a bed of rushes.

The fuzzy shape focused into the face of Peter.

'Are you all right, Andrew?' his brother asked anxiously.

Andrew groaned again but said that yes, he was. However, when he tried to sit up, it was so painful that he decided for the moment at least to remain where he lay.

'Where are we, Pete?' he asked. 'How long have I been unconscious?'

'Not all that long, thank goodness. Only a few minutes really. But I was worried sick, especially when I saw you lying face downwards in the water,' Peter answered.

'Thanks for pulling me out,' Andrew replied ruefully.

'Well, it was that or wait for the water to evaporate,' Peter answered with a wry grin. 'Anyway,' he continued, 'it seems that we're somewhere to the east of the Great Forest, on the other side of the eastern mountains, as far as I can make out. We're with the rest of the Glumps now and this is one of their houses. I dragged you here,' he explained.

'No wonder I'm covered in mud,' said Andrew glancing down at his bedraggled clothes. 'Mind you, it will make me look like one of the Glumps, I suppose. The swamp hog from the bog!'

Peter laughed. 'A sort of mini Earth-Trog – though I never want to meet that creature again, that's for sure! At least the Glumps are friendly, even if they are a bit odd.'

'Well, I suppose it's a good thing we haven't landed in the enemy camp,' Andrew retorted. 'But that was strange, wasn't it? I mean the way we slid down that bank and then . . . well . . . I don't know. The ground just seemed to open up and I felt I was drifting. It was weird. Then suddenly we found ourselves sitting in the middle of a swamp talking to a baby Glump!'

Peter laughed. 'Yes, I mean I don't even know how I slipped. It must have been Elmesh's doing,' he replied. He furrowed his brow. 'I wonder what's happened to Sarah, though. She didn't fall with us. Maybe she hasn't come at all.'

'She'll be very upset if she hasn't,' Andrew answered. 'Still, maybe she's come a different way and we'll meet up later,' he added.

'Well, I hope she's all right,' said Peter, who as her older brother felt responsible for her.

Andrew decided it was time to attempt sitting up again. This time he found it easier.

'So what's it all about, Pete? What were those explosions? Must be some kind of nutter. Whoever is setting them off needs their head examined.'

'I think it's you that needs your head examined,' Peter answered with a laugh. 'But seriously, there's something pretty gruesome going on around here and the Glumps think we're the ones to put a stop to it. The trouble is, I don't see how we can.'

Before he could say more the walls of the room trembled as one of the Glumps waddled, or rather squelched, into the room. When he saw that Andrew was sitting up, he quacked approvingly.

'Ah, good, good. Glad to see you are recovering. Nasty business. Very nasty,' he said.

'This is Mr Glub. Glubble-thunk's dad,' Peter explained.

Andrew nodded.

'Now listen, I don't mind telling you that we are afraid, very afraid indeed,' said Mr Glub. 'And with good reason, as you have already seen. Day and night we are bombarded with rocks, and as if that were not bad enough, they are draining the marshes. If that continues we will be unable to survive and that will be the end of the Glumps. That is why we prayed to Elmesh for help.'

'And are we the help you expected?' Peter queried.

'Why yes, of course. Our wise ones received word from Elmesh that two children of men would come and solve our problems. That is what you are, is it not?'

'Well, yes,' said Peter, who couldn't help noticing that the Glump had referred to only two children coming to the rescue. 'Although we don't usually describe ourselves like that.'

'Just humans, really,' said Andrew.

'That settles it, then. Now can you start as soon as possible and do something about them and their evil plans?' the Glump asked.

Andrew, still feeling dazed, was at a loss.

'Er, yes, I suppose so – maybe. But can you please tell us who your enemies are and why they are harming you?'

'Etins,' replied Mr Glub bluntly. 'Horrible Etins. They are tearing up the countryside to make The Road.'

'I'm sorry, but I still don't understand. What are Etins?' Peter asked.

'You mean you don't know?' The Glump sounded incredulous and made all sorts of glugging and gurgling noises in his throat.

Andrew gazed at his brother and sighed.

'Wouldn't it be nice just for once to have a clue about what we've been let in for before we arrive?' he said.

'We really know nothing about them, except what you've told us,' Peter explained to Mr Glub. 'But you say they're the ones causing all these explosions?' He looked at Andrew, who was feeling the bump on his head again.

'Now that's dangerous all right. No wonder you're scared of them. But don't worry. I expect we can find a way of helping you.' Peter said this with more confidence than he felt. 'The best thing would be for you to take us to where we can get a look at them,' he added.

Mr Glub fairly quivered at the thought.

'I don't think I could do that!' he exclaimed. 'Why, they would crush me underfoot without a second's thought. You don't know what you're asking.'

'Then just show us where they are and we'll go take a look for ourselves,' Peter replied, undaunted by Mr Glub's response.

The Glump gave them one of those don't-say-I-didn't-warn-you looks and said that he hoped they knew what they were doing.

A short while later, Peter and Andrew set off in a northerly direction to find out what all the fuss was about and to get their first sight of Etins. It proved to be very wet work sloshing through the reeds, and they were glad that the shallow water was quite warm.

It took them about twenty minutes to come into sight of the cause of the Glumps' troubles. Fortunately, there were no further explosions during this time, though they continually feared the possibility. What they saw as they peered through the reeds was a mammoth-sized causeway of rock that stretched right across the Bandymarsh. To the east, the causeway disappeared into a far-off smudge of haze; to the west, it ran towards the foot of the mountains beyond which lay the Great Forest.

'Hm, somebody's building a road all right,' Peter observed. 'But who and why? That's the question.'

'Maybe Oswain wants it built. I mean, we don't actually know it's wrong, do we? It's just that the Glumps don't like it,' suggested Andrew, but with very little conviction in his voice.

'Oh yes, I'm sure Oswain would allow people to pelt innocent animals with rocks!' Peter answered with scorn.

'It was only a suggestion,' Andrew retorted, a little piqued by his brother's sarcasm. 'I'm going to take a closer look.'

It took them another fifteen minutes to reach the foot of the causeway. Mostly, this was because they wanted to keep out of sight in case anyone was watching, so they crept through the reeds almost bent double.

The causeway itself was a massive construction built of blasted pieces of rock piled so high that it stood at least three times the boys' own height. Peter thought that it must have taken really heavy machinery to move such great boulders into place.

'Do you reckon it's safe to climb up and take a look?' Andrew asked.

'There doesn't seem to be anybody about,' Peter observed. 'I guess we'll get a better view from the top.' He made up his mind. 'Come on then, but keep your eyes open for trouble.'

The road proved to be wide and was finished with carefully laid blocks of stone. The boys gazed at it in amazement. Whoever had built it must be wanting to move either a very large army or to drive heavy vehicles along it. Then they noticed a huge lake on the other side. It was obvious that the causeway was damming the water that flowed down from the northern mountains. By comparison, the marshlands from which Peter and Andrew had come looked very sparse.

'No wonder the Glumps are running out of water,' said Andrew. 'It's all being trapped up here.'

'What I can't understand is why they don't just move to the other side, then,' said Peter. 'I mean . . .'

He never finished his sentence, for suddenly they felt the ground tremble beneath their feet. Both looked around in alarm. A huge cloud of dust was rapidly approaching where they stood.

'Quick!' gasped Peter. 'Run for it! Down the side.'

In haste they tumbled and scrambled off the causeway to the marshes below. The next moment, a deep rumble filled the air. A column of simply monstrous creatures came thundering into view. They were moving at great speed and pushing enormous wheelbarrows filled with massive boulders.

Peter and Andrew cowered among the rocks below. They gazed up in awe as the grey, shaggy-haired giants hurtled past. As tall as trees, bulging with muscle and with fierce looks on their faces, nothing would stand in their path.

'I think we've just met the Etins,' Peter whispered grimly.

'Now I know why the Glumps are afraid,' said Andrew with feeling. 'So am I! And they're expecting us to stop them? They've got to be joking!'

* * *

Sarah strode glumly along the path accompanied by her escort, Banter. This wasn't at all like the Great Forest she knew and loved.

Now that the magistrates had pronounced their verdict on Sarah, Banter seemed more relaxed. He talked non-stop about the way they were trying to improve the health and safety of the forest. It appeared that they had committees for all sorts of things, from path clearance to the right kind of wood for building houses. Everybody was busy 'tidying up the mess', as he called it.

Sarah sighed and wished he would be quiet.

'But why are you doing all this?' she exclaimed in exasperation. 'I mean, it never used to be like this before.' She pointed to a rabbit busily sweeping the path with a besom broom. 'Why do you need to do that? What's wrong with leaving things as they are? Is this what Oswain really wants?'

'I don't know about that, miss,' Banter replied honestly. 'The King has been absent for a long time. Some say he's dead, or lost – or even that he's abandoned us. That's why we formed the republic.'

'That can't be true,' Sarah exclaimed, her eyes wide with horror at the thought. 'And I'm sure he doesn't like things done in this way.'

'Well, that's the way it is,' said the hare firmly. 'And don't you go causing me any trouble with ideas to the contrary. Otherwise I'll have to report you.'

Sarah went quiet. There was something wrong with the forest and nobody was saying what it was. She decided then and there that she would have to get away from her guard and find out for herself. Somehow she must reach Trotter.

Her chance came sooner than she expected.

They were walking along one of the paths that took them towards a row of neatly kept cottages, each with a very tidy fenced garden. Suddenly there was a commotion.

'I've been burgled!' screamed a voice. The next moment, a very irate rat came storming out of his front door.

'Those vermin are about again,' he yelled to nobody in particular. Then, spotting Sarah and Banter, he stomped towards them waving his paw angrily.

'I thought you were supposed to stop this sort of thing,' he shouted at Banter. 'What's the use of having forest guards if you don't do your job properly?'

The commotion brought all the neighbours onto the path. They swarmed around Banter, demanding to know what was going to be done about the spate of burglaries in their district.

Carefully, Sarah edged her way to the outskirts of the crowd. Then, while her guard was distracted, she slipped unnoticed into the undergrowth, and ran for all she was worth.

'Whew, thank goodness for that!' she puffed, coming to a rest after a few minutes. 'Now to find some of my old friends, if I can.'

Sarah realised at once that she must be careful. No doubt someone would raise the alarm as soon as they discovered that she was missing. Somebody might even think she was the thief, or in league with him. It astonished her to realise that she was a fugitive in the Great Forest.

However, Sarah knew exactly what to do. 'I must make for the Enchanted Glade. I bet that's where I'll find Trotter. Perhaps I'll get to look into the Star Pool as well. Then I'll really know what's going on,' she said to herself.

Long ago, Sarah and her brothers had helped Oswain rid the forest of an evil Shadow-witch named Hagbane. The witch had stolen the Merestone that gave the forest its life and beauty. After they had won the battle, the victors put the jewel back where it belonged in the Enchanted Glade. It rested beside Elmere, the Star Pool. If you gazed into the pool with a true heart, the waters would reveal visions of what you needed to know.*

Of course, Sarah at this time had no idea where she was in the vastness of the Great Forest. All she knew was that she was somewhere far to the south, so would have to travel northwards. 'Elmesh, please help me,' she half-prayed. Then she set off in what she hoped was the right direction.

Sarah walked and occasionally jogged for the rest of that day, stopping only once or twice to eat some berries

---

*You can read all about this in *Oswain and the Battle for Alamore*.

and to drink from the occasional small stream. She grew weary as the day dragged on. Already she had crossed a number of the well-guarded paths and on one occasion she almost stumbled from the undergrowth right onto one of the red-barred barriers. Fortunately, the guards were busy talking and failed to hear her, but she was even more careful after this.

At length, hungry and tired as the evening shadows began to fall, she came upon a small hamlet. There seemed to be plenty of animals about and she pondered whether it would be safe to mingle with them. Perhaps someone could answer her questions.

She had just taken a step into the open when someone shouted with alarm, 'Enemy! The enemy is about!'

Sarah at once turned on her heels and ran for her life into what she hoped was the safety of the undergrowth. As nobody followed her, she realised that the forest-folk felt afraid of being off the paths. It was some comfort for her, but only increased her sense of loneliness and isolation. As dusk fell, she began to despair. Was there nobody she could trust?

'This is awful,' she exclaimed aloud. 'And in the Great Forest too! What's happened to everyone? Don't they trust Elmesh any more? Why are they so afraid?'

'Not everyone is like that, child.'

Sarah jumped at the sudden sound. Looking this way and that, she tried to find out where the voice had come from, but could see nobody there.

'Who are you?' she gasped. 'Where are you?'

'Over here,' the voice replied softly.

It was then that Sarah spotted a hedgehog curled up by a tree root. She went across and the hedgehog unrolled himself. He had a kindly face.

'What is your name?' he asked.

'Sarah,' she replied.

'You had better come with me, Sarah. I think I can help you.'

'Are you loyal to Oswain and to Elmesh?' she asked suspiciously, as she prepared to run.

'More than you will ever know,' the hedgehog answered. There was an unmistakable tinge of respect in his voice.

Sarah sighed with relief and she felt tears start in her eyes.

'Thank goodness for that! I thought the whole place had gone mad.'

'Perhaps it has,' said the hedgehog. 'But William and his missus haven't, that's for sure.'

The hedgehog led Sarah along a narrow winding track. It was so gloomy by now that she could scarcely see her way.

They stopped at the door of a small house built into the root of a tree. To Sarah's amazement, glinting in the last remains of the light, she saw fixed to the door the small figure of a white eagle.

'Arca!' she breathed.

4

The Guild of the White Eagle

'Yes,' said the hedgehog knowingly. 'It is Arca, indeed. At least, it's our image of him – though many folk down this way seem to think that it's no more than a good-luck charm.'

Sarah smiled to herself, then said, 'I once rode on Arca's back into battle. He saved me from being killed.' Her voice grew distant as she spoke. 'It was the most wonderful experience of my life. I can still feel the wind beneath his wings. He's so powerful! How could anyone treat him like a good-luck charm?'

She turned to face the hedgehog. He was staring at her in absolute open-mouthed amazement.

'Do you mean to say you are *that* Sarah?' he asked in hushed tones. 'I'm sorry . . . if I had known . . . oh, please forgive me for not being more polite. But this is amazing,' he stammered. 'Oh, do come in. You must meet my wife at once.'

'Yes,' said Sarah, somewhat taken aback by his response. 'But I'm nobody special really.'

'Nobody special?' exclaimed the hedgehog. 'You are nothing less than a legend among the members of our Guild! We recite the tales of your deeds almost every time we meet. And here you are right on our doorstep!'

Sarah marvelled to think that folk met together to tell stories about her exploits. Yet even greater was her relief at finding someone she could trust. The hedgehog opened the door and with great politeness ushered her over the threshold. She accepted gladly.

'Is that you, William?' came a voice from inside.

'It is, my dear, and I've brought a guest. Someone very special indeed.'

'Oh me, Oh my, what have you been up to now?' said Mrs Hedgehog. 'And no warning as usual!' She bustled into the room carrying a tray full of crockery. 'Oh, goodness gracious me!' she exclaimed when she saw Sarah. 'Who on earth is this?'

The tray tilted alarmingly.

'Hello,' said Sarah. 'I'm sorry to barge in on you like this, but . . .'

'Oh, don't worry, my dear. William is always bringing folk home at short notice. Though I must say he's never invited a child of man back before. That's what took me by surprise.' She viewed her husband quizzically as she put the tray on the table.

'Mary,' said William solemnly, 'this is no less a person than Sarah of the White Eagle.'

Mary's mouth gaped open as though she could hardly believe her ears.

'*The* Sarah, you mean?'

'Absolutely,' said William with a pleased smile.

'Well I never! Sit down, my dear. And please excuse our humble abode. We've never had anyone famous visiting this house before.' She looked at her husband. 'I wish you had told me, William. Just look at the mess the place is in!'

Sarah protested that everything was fine and took the seat that William offered.

The hedgehogs' house had a wonderful warm, earthy atmosphere. Garlands of acorns and dried berries hung from the rafters and dried leaves decorated the walls. A copper oil lamp cast a mellow glow across the oak table above which it hung. The floor was dusted with straw. Sarah felt relaxed for the first time since arriving in the Great Forest.

'We weren't due to have a meeting of the Guild until next week,' said William. 'But now that you are here we simply must have one tonight. I'll start the message off at once. You had better give our honoured guest something to eat, Mary. I won't be gone long.'

Without further ado, William slipped out of the door.

'Excuse me. I hope you don't mind my asking, but I don't understand about this Guild. What is it? And who are you all?' Sarah enquired.

'Oh dear!' replied Mary. 'Didn't that silly husband of mine tell you anything? Well, I'd better explain then.'

Mary busied herself laying the table as she spoke. Sarah was ravenous and her mouth drooled as milk, cheese, bread and cakes arrived from the kitchen.

'We are a special society,' explained the hedgehog. 'We meet because we honour the memory and the name of Arca. That's why we call ourselves the Guild of the White Eagle. We keep alive the story of his adventures. We also tell the tale of the romance of our King – may

Elmesh rest his soul – and of the Ice Maiden. Of course, we also know all about the part played by the three children of men – the children who helped rescue the Great Forest from the Shadow-witch.'

'That was my two brothers, Peter and Andrew, and me. It was our first adventure,' Sarah explained. 'We've had several others since then.'

'I still cannot get over you being here,' said Mary. 'It's like one of the stories has come alive. It's amazing! You must excuse me if I seem a little bit flustered.'

Sarah assured her that it was quite all right.

Mary smiled. 'Well, it all happened in the northern part of the forest, as you probably know. We were glad when things changed for the better, but the events never really affected us down here. Besides, some of our Guild were too young to remember.' She poured Sarah a glass of milk and encouraged her to tuck in.

'So have you never met Arca, or Oswain or Loriana, or Trotter?' Sarah asked as she helped herself to bread and jam.

'No, I have never seen Arca, nor has my husband and nor, as far as I know, has anyone else in our Guild. And as for the King, well, we don't know what has become of him. It is a very sad affair.'

Sarah's face clouded. Just what had happened to Oswain?

William's return interrupted their conversation.

'It's all done,' he puffed. 'The message has gone round.' Then addressing Sarah he said, 'Oh good, you're getting enough to eat, I hope. I trust my wife is looking after you.'

Sarah laughed and said that she was being very well fed indeed and was extremely grateful.

She had just finished eating when the first of the guests arrived. It was a rabbit. A pair of squirrels quickly followed; then a weasel and a dormouse. Each one stared at Sarah in amazement as they entered.

Before long a company of about twenty animals had squeezed into William and Mary's house. William started the proceedings.

'As you know,' he said, 'we are only a small group of outcasts and most of the other forest-folk around here think that we are foolish to live as we do. Some even doubt our loyalty. Tonight, it is my pleasure to introduce to you someone who can tell the truth about Arca from her own experience. She knows him personally and has even ridden on his back!'

He introduced Sarah with great ceremony.

The gathered company applauded her. It was obvious that she was meant to make a little speech.

'I don't really know what to say,' she began. 'But I am grateful for your kind welcome. Elmesh has brought me back to the Great Forest for a reason that I don't yet know. But . . . but things are very different and I have never been to this part before. Something seems terribly wrong, because the Great Forest should be full of happiness. Instead, everyone seems afraid. I don't understand about the barriers and the guards and why people are so miserable. It never used to be like this. So can anyone please tell me what's going on? And why are you people different?'

'Everyone's frightened,' muttered one of the squirrels. 'They're afraid of the danger.'

'What danger?' asked Sarah.

'There's trouble in the forest all right,' piped up the dormouse. 'Forest-folk have even been killed. Somebody's out there stalking us. A human being, that's what. Somebody with a bow and arrow, who shoots to kill. It's so frightening and there seems to be nobody to help us.'

'But what about Trotter and Stiggle, and Fumble, Mumble and Grumble, and all the people I used to know?' began Sarah.

'Oh, they are still alive, so we hear, but they live far to the north and they are very old,' explained a young vole.

'But doesn't anybody else know what to do?'

'No,' said William sadly. 'When the troubles began we thought we should seek help from the Merestone. But some of those in charge said that was wrong and super-stitious and old-fashioned, and that we must organise our own defences. Elmesh would only help those who help themselves. So they formed the republic and began to make rules and committees and to keep people on safe paths in the hope that they could control what was happening.'

'It hasn't worked, of course,' said Mary. 'All it's done is to make life difficult for everybody. Do you know, they actually forbid us to walk off the paths and into the undergrowth?'

'But you don't keep the rules, do you?' said Sarah. 'Otherwise you would have reported me.'

'That's because we still believe in the old ways,' explained the rabbit. 'But they don't like us meeting and talking like this. They treat us like outcasts and they're very suspicious of us. One day they'll pass a rule to ban us meeting all together!'

'That's why we have this symbol of a white eagle,' explained the squirrel who hadn't yet spoken. 'It's a way of recognising one another.'

'It all sounds terrible,' said Sarah. 'Nobody should be an outcast in the Great Forest. So who makes all these rules and regulations?'

'Oh, it's a committee, the people's committee, but it's mostly made up of hares. They decide, always for our own good of course. But we hate it. We'd sooner trust Elmesh and hope for the best,' said the weasel.

'Hear, hear,' cried the others.

Sarah stood to her feet. She was earnest. 'Listen, I think you're very brave and good people and I'm glad you trust me, because I now know how dangerous it is for you to trust a . . . a human being.' She felt a bit choked up and paused. 'Elmesh has brought me here because of this problem. I don't know what to do yet, but I believe I must find Trotter and talk with him. You are the only ones I can trust, so can you help me, please? I need to reach the Enchanted Glade. Does anyone know how to get there? I think it's really urgent.'

William spoke. 'We would feel very honoured to help in any way we can,' he said. 'It's the least we can do.'

'I think I know the way,' said the weasel. 'You see, Stiggle is my great uncle and I can probably remember where he lives, or at least where he used to live. And the Enchanted Glade isn't far from there. I visited him once,' he explained.

'We must go at once,' said William. 'It'll be safer travelling in the dark than in the daylight.'

'Yes,' said Sarah. 'Especially as they are treating me as one of the enemy and they're now hunting me like some kind of criminal. I dread to think what would happen if I got caught.'

'There is one more matter before you go,' said William. 'I'm sure I speak for everyone when I say we would like you to become an honorary member of the Guild.'

Sarah was delighted. So with smiles all round they presented her with a badge which she pinned to her sweatshirt. 'Because I haven't got a door to put it on,' she explained.

So it was that Sarah set off on the long journey to the Enchanted Glade accompanied by William and the weasel, whose name was Taril. Everyone in the Guild wished them good speed and a safe journey.

It was very dark in the forest and it took quite a long time for Sarah's eyes to adjust to the shadowy trees and shrubs. Led by Taril, they followed paths that were winding and narrow. Sarah knew she would be instantly lost without her guides and realised that apart from their help she would never reach the Enchanted Glade. So skilful was the weasel, that only once or twice did they cross one of the main paths and that was nowhere near any of the guard-posts.

However, Sarah began to feel uncomfortable. She had

the uncanny sense that she was being watched or followed. Maybe both. Once or twice she even turned round quickly and fancied she saw a shadow flitting in the dark undergrowth. It was rather unnerving and she mentioned it to her companions.

'That's the trouble,' said William. 'Nobody knows who's who. Hardly anyone trusts anyone else these days. There are shadows everywhere. Strange people pass through the forest. Forest-folk are killed and nobody knows who's done it. These are truly dangerous times.'

Sarah shivered and hastened her footsteps. She prayed that they would get to the Enchanted Glade in safety.

The journey took them two days. Because of the danger the three fugitives slept during the daylight hours and travelled only at night. It was almost dawn on the third night of their journey when Taril stopped. He pointed to a small door built into a bank.

'That's where my great uncle Stiggle used to live,' he said.

They approached the door and knocked, but it swung open of its own accord. It was obvious that the place was deserted.

'He's gone, I guess', said Taril with a shrug of disappointment. 'Like so many these days. I don't know where he might be. Nor do I know where to go from here, because I've never been any further. From now on we will just have to trust that we find our way.'

Sarah stood stock still. She sensed something in the

air. Some invisible power caressed her senses, a faint tremor like the lightest of summer breezes on a bare arm, but it was unmistakable.

'I think I could find the way now!' she exclaimed. 'I can feel the nearness of the Merestone.'

Her companions looked at her in amazement but were very happy to let her lead. Sarah moved confidently along the narrow paths as they twisted and turned through the trees. At last she saw the sign she had been looking for. Two large sentinel stones marked the entrance to the Enchanted Glade.

'There it is!' she exclaimed, and she broke into a run.

The others hastened forward until they stood with her on the threshold of the glade. The air itself seemed to tingle with mystery, and it breathed the most wonderful fragrance. At once Sarah felt her tiredness depart. She gazed across the glade at the beauty of the muted shadows. Then, high in the sky, shining clearly like a gleaming drop of dew hanging in the heavens, she saw Elrilion, the star of Elmesh. Sarah let out a sigh of relief and then, followed by her companions, walked quietly into the glade.

Ahead of her, she knew, lay the Star Pool, known as Elmere. A faint silvery glow above the trees betrayed its presence. Sarah made straight towards it.

Then, to her unbounded joy, she saw the figure of a very, very ancient badger. He was bent almost double and leaned heavily on a stick. But he was waiting for her. In the starlight she caught the gleam of his eye as he lifted his head to face her.

'Sarah,' quavered the voice. 'You've come! I've been waiting for you.'

With tears in her eyes Sarah ran forward with her arms opened wide.

'Trotter, Trotter, it's you!' she exclaimed. 'Thank goodness I've found you!'

She flung her arms around the aged badger and hugged him for all she was worth.

5

Into the Enemy Camp

Peter and Andrew were tangled up in their own adventures beyond the eastern mountains.

'Well, what do you make of that lot?' said Peter to his brother, as the Etins thundered past them and disappeared into the distance in a cloud of dust.

'Dunno,' said Andrew glumly. He sat on a boulder with his chin cupped in his hands. 'I mean, how do we stop giants like that? And what do we do about this road? There's no way we can take it apart, is there? We couldn't even make a hole in it to let the water run back into the marshes. It just seems so impossible.'

'But surely we've got to do something,' Peter protested. 'I mean, Elmesh must have brought us here to help the Glubs get their water back, so we've got to try. We can't just sit here doing nothing all day, can we?'

'All right, give me the dynamite, then, and we'll blow it up!' Andrew retorted sarcastically.

'Don't be stupid!'

'Well, you think of something better, 'cos I'm not going back to the Glubs to say "sorry, we can't help you",' said Andrew. 'Let's face it, Pete, they really think we're going to solve their problems, but we haven't a clue how to do it!'

'Why don't we follow the Etins, then?' Peter suggested. 'At least we could find out what they're doing and how many there are. Maybe that's the way we'll get some clues. You never know, something might turn up to help us.'

Reluctantly Andrew agreed.

They decided to follow the Etins westwards in the direction of the mountains. It looked the shorter distance, and they knew that was where the Etins must be working. They agreed that at the first sign of trouble they would scramble off the road again and hope that they could hide.

It was a very hot day and the sun beat down remorselessly on the grey surface of the road. After an hour's walking, both boys felt so tired that they no longer bothered to listen out for the Etins. It was all they could do to keep plodding on.

'This road seems to go on for ever,' gasped Andrew. 'When will we reach the end?'

Peter stopped and looked around him. In either direction the road vanished into the haze of the afternoon heat. On their right hand side the dammed-up water gleamed in the sunlight. At least dying of thirst would not be their problem, Peter thought.

'Better keep walking,' he muttered. 'There's no sense giving up in the middle of nowhere!'

It was late afternoon when they finally saw what they were looking for. They had come so far along the road that it was beginning to rise through a pass at the foot of the mountains. The waters of the marshlands had given way to forest. Wantonly smashed trees littered each side of the causeway. Such was the careless violence of the builders.

Ahead of them they saw the Etins.

'We'd better get off the road,' said Peter grimly.

Andrew agreed, so for the last part of their journey the two boys moved with stealth among the fallen trees and undergrowth. What they saw as they drew closer simply amazed them. There were dozens of enormous Etins busily laying the road. They grabbed gigantic boulders as though they weighed no more than large stones and then, with resounding crashes, they simply slammed them into place.

Some of the Etins were tearing great chunks of stone from the sides of the mountain and carrying them down to the causeway. Others stomped on the road so hard that their enormous weight crushed slabs of rock into place to make a level surface. The noise was deafening and clouds of dust rose all around. Peter and Andrew had little likelihood of being spotted in the midst of all this chaos so they were able to get quite close. Peering through the dust cloud they could see other Etins striding ahead using their great arms as flails to smash aside the trees as though they were no more than matchwood.

It was an awesome sight and did nothing to lift Peter and Andrew's spirits. How could they possibly stop these juggernauts? They watched in glum silence as the work progressed. Then suddenly, as it was nearing dusk, one of the Etins let out a loud 'Woaaarrgh!' It was the signal for work to cease, and quickly the Etins gathered on the road, together with their wheelbarrows.

'A good day's work, gang,' thundered the Etin who was obviously the foreman of the party. 'Our lord will be pleased. Tomorrow his kingdom will come another day's journey on the road we have built.'

The other Etins growled their approval.

'Nothing will halt the triumph of Feldrog, the Eternal Master!' cried the foreman.

'Nothing!' roared the Etins in response.

Peter and Andrew were by now hiding behind some fallen trees quite close to the gang. They could hear everything clearly.

'So that's their game,' said Peter. 'This Feldrog, who-ever he is, is making a road so that he can bring his kingdom along it. I wonder what that means?'

'Then that's why we're here,' exclaimed Andrew as the penny dropped. 'We've got to stop this Feldrog guy, before he reaches the Great Forest. If we can do that, the Glubs won't have any problems anyway, because then we can get help to break up the dam.'

'The question is, how do we stop them? I mean, it's no easier, now we've found out what's really going on,' said Peter. He frowned. 'I wonder if Oswain and Loriana know about it. Perhaps they're already waiting for them on the other side of the mountains.'

'Maybe they've got an army together and there's going to be a big showdown,' suggested Andrew.

'Hmm,' said Peter. 'You might be right. But if Elmesh has sent us here, to this side of the mountain, there must be a reason for it.'

While they were pondering what they should do, the Etins were putting their tools into their wheelbarrows. They were obviously preparing to return along the road. Peter watched them thoughtfully.

'I've got a plan,' he said. 'Why don't we find out where their camp is? We can't do anything here, and it would take us too long to get across the mountains to warn Oswain – even if we're meant to.'

'But it will take us just as long to reach their camp,' Andrew protested. 'I mean, how many miles is it? It's taken us all afternoon just to get this far.'

'That's where my idea comes in. We could travel by wheelbarrow,' said Peter excitedly.

'By wheelbarrow?' Andrew repeated incredulously. 'You mean up there?' He gestured towards the road above them.

'Yes,' said Peter. 'Look, we're so small they'd hardly notice us, would they? Anyway, I reckon we could sit on the frame thing underneath and be completely hidden. That's the only way we'll travel at any speed around here. Let's face it.'

Andrew looked at his brother as though he had gone completely mad. The Etins would probably eat them if they were caught! It was a crazy idea, but what else could they do? 'All right,' he said. 'Let's give it a go!'

So, as the gloom thickened, the two boys clambered up onto the road, keeping as much out of sight as possible. Nobody noticed them, and soon they were standing at the foot of one of the giant wheels. It was obvious that they didn't have much time. The Etins were preparing to leave and already some were holding their wheel-barrow handles.

Quickly Peter and Andrew scrambled up the spokes of a wheel and then onto the axle. They ran across, balancing precariously, until they reached the frame of the barrow. There they found an angle between two spars where they could sit and hang on. Being underneath, they were well out of sight of the Etins.

'Made it!' gasped Peter. His eyes were bright with excitement.

They were not a moment too soon. With a cry from the foreman, the Etins began to move forward with their barrows. The pace picked up very quickly and soon they were running at tremendous speed. Peter and Andrew hung on for dear life as their wheelbarrow bounced along the road.

The Etins moved at an incredible pace, taking massive thunderous strides without any apparent effort. They created such a cloud of dust that Andrew and Peter could barely see where they were going and they wished they had climbed onto one of the barrows at the front of the gang rather than in the middle.

As the sun set, they passed the mournful marshlands and could dimly make out the lake. Then the terrain changed to open moorland that looked desolate and bleak in the fading light. The boys' arms began to ache and they felt as if every bone in their bodies was being jarred out of joint. It was impossible to speak above the rumble of the wheelbarrows and the crashing of the giants' feet.

Soon it was almost completely dark. The Etins raced tirelessly on into the night.

It might have been a chunk of rock in the road. Maybe Peter's concentration lapsed. Whatever the reason, the wheelbarrow suddenly jolted violently and Peter lost his grip. In sudden panic he tried desperately to hang on, but it was no good. With a cry of alarm, he was thrown from his perch and sent spinning through the air. The next moment, he hit the ground with a sickening thud. It was all over in a second.

Andrew cried out but there was nothing he could do. Already the Etins were hundreds of metres down the road from where his brother had fallen. He thought about jumping off, but he knew he didn't have the nerve to do so. Sick with worry, he could only cling grimly to the frame of the wheelbarrow as it careered into the gloom.

* * *

In fact, Andrew's nightmare journey ended sooner than he expected. After about ten minutes, he saw a blaze of light ahead. He huddled down tight against the spar onto which he was holding, and wished he had the power to make himself invisible. The next moment, they were on the outskirts of what looked to be a vast encampment. The Etins came to a halt on the outskirts and without further ado dropped their wheelbarrows and stomped off to their own affairs.

Slowly and painfully, Andrew eased his stiffened limbs and climbed down from his perch. He was cold and covered from head to foot in dust. He licked his parched lips and wondered where he could get a drink. Every joint in his body ached and he was hungry too.

'What a mess!' he said to himself.

He felt very lonely without his brother and just hoped that Peter wasn't badly injured. Observing that the coast was clear he ran from the shadow of the wheelbarrow and slipped behind one of the many tents that made up the encampment. So far, nobody had spotted him.

The light came from bright globes that hung from poles like Chinese lanterns. There were simply hundreds of them so that the whole area was ablaze with light. Andrew decided he would try to get closer to the centre and find out what was going on. Cautiously he slipped behind another tent.

What happened next Andrew could never have predicted. To his complete amazement, everything around him instantly vanished. He found himself standing on the open road under a starlit sky. The experience completely unnerved him and he had to pinch himself to see if it was true. He even tried putting a hand over each eye in turn. It made no difference. The camp had simply vanished.

Warily, he began to walk along the road. He could see no signs of life whatsoever.

He was just wondering what to do next, when as suddenly as it had vanished, the entire camp reappeared. Only this time Andrew stood fully exposed to sight right in the middle of it. Before he could so much as react, he was thrown to the ground as though struck by lightning. Pain coursed through his body.

Then a voice spoke into his mind. He could not say what the words were, but a terrible fear fell upon him as he listened. It was a fear so deep that he knew he would obey the owner of that voice without question. Slowly he raised his head. The sight that confronted him took his breath away.

* * *

Meanwhile Peter had picked himself up from the ground. He felt very dazed and he hurt all over. Gingerly he felt for signs of broken bones. Thankfully he found none, but the bruises made him wince. He realised that he had narrowly escaped being crushed to death under the wheelbarrows and the thundering feet of the Etins. Then he discovered why. He was no longer on the road. Looking up, he could see the outline of the causeway. As far as he could make out in the faint light, he had fallen down a steep grassy embankment and was standing on the edge of some dark woodlands.

Gloomily he faced the fact that he was stranded in the middle of nowhere. With an effort he climbed back onto the road, but in either direction there was nothing but darkness. If the Etins had a camp, it was a very, very long way off. He was tempted for a moment to follow them but quickly realised that it would be fruitless.

Worried sick about Andrew he clambered off the road for safety.

At that moment, despair all but overwhelmed him and he felt like crying. His brother Andrew might be in terrible danger by now and he had no way of helping him. He did not know whether his sister was even in Oswain's realm. He felt terribly lonely and dispirited.

Then he looked up. The first stars were appearing, and there hanging low on the horizon was Elrilion. The star of Elmesh shone sharp and clear like a diamond against the velvet backdrop. Peter stared at it for a long while and as he did so his spirits began steadily to rise. There was hope in the darkness. Somehow things would work out all right after all.

Greatly encouraged he decided that he would shelter in the woods for the night and work out what to do the next morning.

By the pale light of the stars he walked among the trees looking for a suitable spot. Finding a dark shape that looked comfortable, he sat down and leaned against it.

It was then that Peter got the shock of his life.

'Oi,' said an indignant voice. 'Mind where you're leaning.'

Peter almost jumped out of his skin. He leapt to his feet and stumbled against another tree.

'Me too,' said the tree. 'Who do you think you are, barging into innocent folk like that?'

'Without any "by your leaf" either,' retorted the first tree.

The other one made a chortling noise.

Peter looked around him. He was frightened out of his wits. His first instinct was to run, but he saw that glowing eyes were watching him on all sides.

'I-I'm sorry,' he stammered. 'I didn't realise. Who-who are you?'

In spite of the shock, Peter didn't feel any terrible sense of evil. With an effort of will he overcame the temptation to flee for his life.

'Who are we?' replied a woody voice. 'I'll tell you who we are. We're the Barkums.'

'Yes,' added another voice. 'We've got branches everywhere.'

'I've never heard of you,' said Peter.

'Perhaps that's because you haven't twigged who we are,' said the first voice. 'Still, you don't look like a threat to leaf or limb. Tell us who you are.'

'I'm Peter, Peter Brown.'

'Ooo, I like the name Brown. It has a real barky feel about it,' said the first voice. 'My name's Oakum.'

'And I'm Sycum,' said the other voice.

'I'm very pleased to meet you, and I'm sorry I disturbed you,' said Peter apologetically.

'Oh, you needn't be too sorry,' said Oakum. 'But you'd better tell us more about yourself and whose side you're on.'

'I don't understand,' said Peter. 'Except that I'm not on the side of those Etins.'

'I should think not too,' said Oakum in a strong voice. 'They are very wicked. They are destroying the trees to make their awful road.'

'I can see that,' said Peter. 'In fact, er . . . I've been sent to . . . er . . . to stop them.'

'Well, we'll be rooting for you, if that's what you want to do,' replied Sycum.

'Oh, that's a corny joke,' chortled Oakum.

Peter laughed. 'Well, I don't know how I'm going to do it. I was with my brother, Andrew, but we've got separated,' he said.

'Well, maybe you've fallen among friends,' said Oakum.

While this conversation was taking place, Peter's eyes were growing accustomed to the gloom. Gradually he found he could make out the shape of these strange creatures. At first sight they seemed to be a part of the trees they stood against. Then he realised that they were somewhat thinner, and they were faintly luminous in the dark. Their eyes were bright and their slightly sad-looking woody faces were friendly. They did not appear old, but Peter gained the impression that they had lived a very long time.

'Well, I'm glad you think I'm all right,' he said, 'because honestly I am. I'm a servant of Elmesh and I'm a friend of Oswain's.'

'Oh, then that's very good,' said Sycum. 'We will certainly do what we can to help you.'

'What kind of folk are you?' enquired Peter.

'Us? We are the Barkums but some folk call us tree nymphs.'

At that moment Peter saw a pair of eyes moving

towards him. He realised then that the tree nymphs could walk. At first he had thought they were joined to the trees.

'Oh hello, Birchum Tenokum,' said Oakum. 'Come and meet Peter. He's an enemy of the Etins.'

This Barkum was very well spoken. 'Oh good,' he said. 'Then we must join forces and think of a plan to assist you. What is your problem?'

Peter quickly explained his predicament.

As he spoke, the Barkums made sighing noises like a soft wind in the trees.

'I don't like them at all, and whoever this Feldrog is, he sounds very sinister,' Peter concluded.

'Hear, hear,' cried all the Barkums, and they made a sound like the rattling of many branches in a storm.

'We bow to nobody,' exclaimed Birchum. 'Elmesh is our only master.'

'Those Etins will be barking up the wrong tree if they think they can take us on,' said Sycum.

'They ain't see'd nothing,' growled another Barkum who had just appeared on the scene.

'Oh it's you, Alderum,' said Oakum. 'Come and meet Peter. We're going to work together to root out those Etins.'

'Well, shiver me timbers!' exclaimed Alderum.

Peter laughed with the others. He felt really at home with these strange creatures and their odd puns. With their help he hoped he would find Andrew. Then they could tackle the Etins. As for this Feldrog, well, he was no big deal!

6

The Enchanted Glade

Sarah quickly introduced to Trotter her new-found friends, William and Taril. The hedgehog and the weasel seemed to be at a loss for words. Lord Trotter's fame was legendary, and here he was standing before them in no less a place than the Enchanted Glade itself.

'Pl-pleased to meet you, sir,' stammered William. 'Thank you for seeing us.'

Taril bowed low and mumbled something about it being a great honour.

However, Trotter soon put his guests at ease and made them feel really welcome by asking them all about themselves. He was fascinated to learn about the Guild of the White Eagle. When William said that it seemed that all the tales they had told were suddenly coming to life, the badger chuckled.

'True tales never die,' he said knowingly. 'Like me they just grow a little older.'

Taril told Trotter that Stiggle was his relative and asked after him.

'Well, you will meet your great uncle soon enough,' said Trotter. 'Stiggle lives here deep in the glade. Asleep at the moment, of course. Like all the others.' His mood became suddenly thoughtful and he added, 'I don't sleep much myself these days. Watching and waiting. Just watching and waiting.'

His words reminded Sarah why she was here. 'What do you mean?' she asked in a voice that betrayed her anxiety. 'Trotter, just what is going on in the Great Forest? Something is very wrong, isn't it? And what has happened to Oswain and Loriana? Where is everyone? Where is Mrs Trotter?'

The old badger coughed and gave her a sad look. 'Ah, Sarah, you may well ask. Indeed, things are bad. Worse than I have known them for a long time.' He motioned with his paw. 'Come this way, all of you, and I will explain as best I can. I need to rest my weary old legs.'

Trotter led them from the threshold of the Enchanted Glade to an open space. There they found a small circle of logs where they could sit down. The starlight caught a faraway look in his eyes as he began to speak.

'It has been coming for a long time, of course. Maybe for as long as the tales have ever been told. The signs were always there for those with eyes to see them.' He nodded and sighed. 'Hmm, but now the end is near. The world cannot continue as it is, that much is certain.'

Sarah looked at him with alarm. 'What on earth do you mean?' she exclaimed.

'I mean we have reached a time of trouble that will mark the end . . . and the beginning,' he answered cryptically. 'Things are drawing towards their climax. True enough, everything will be renewed, but the cracks in the old order of things must first grow wider.'

As he spoke, Sarah grew increasingly apprehensive.

Trotter's mood was strange. She began to wonder whether old age was taking its toll and the badger was growing a bit simple in the head. William and Taril just sat with blank expressions on their faces.

'Trotter, you're speaking in riddles,' she cried. 'Listen, Elmesh has brought me back to the Great Forest. It's the thing I most wanted to happen. All right, so I arrived somewhere to the south where things are different. But something terrible is going on down there. The animals are frightened. They're behaving like . . . like secret police,' she exclaimed and waved her hands in exasperation. 'I was arrested and ordered out under an armed escort. They think I'm the enemy! Then I hear that Oswain has vanished and so has Loriana, and then there's this . . . this republic stuff. There's even talk of someone going around shooting the forest-folk with arrows.' She drew a deep breath. 'It's just so awful, and I don't even know where my two brothers are. For all I know they might . . . might be dead as well.'

With that, Sarah began to cry. 'This is not what I expected at all,' she sobbed. 'I thought it would be wonderful to be back in the Great Forest. But now I think I just want to go home.'

The badger laid a comforting paw on her arm. She could feel him trembling slightly.

'Sarah, I am sorry that you feel like this, and I do understand,' he said with sympathy. 'I too am distressed by the state of things. Do you think I am unaware of events in the forest? True, I did not know of our noble friends and their Guild – he nodded in William and

Taril's direction – but I know only too well the danger that lurks out there. It . . . it cost me the life of my dear wife,' he faltered.

Sarah gasped. Her hand flew to her mouth and her eyes started with shock. 'No! Oh, no! It can't be,' she exclaimed. Fresh tears poured down her cheeks.

The aged badger nodded his head. 'It happened just over a year ago,' he explained. 'She had gone to visit old Sally Mole down by Aldred's Park. When she arrived – according to eyewitnesses – there was a great commotion because Sally had been shot. There she was, lying on the grass pierced through with an arrow.'

'Wh-what happened?' Sarah stammered.

Trotter raised his eyes to hers and gave the hint of a wry smile. 'Typical of my wife, I suppose. Ignoring any danger to herself she sent packing all those who had come out to see what had happened.' He paused. 'She was the last one to leave. There was another arrow, and it took her life.'

Sarah reached out her hand. 'I-I'm so sorry,' she said. 'It's just so awful.'

The badger shrugged. 'Not just for me, though I feel it badly enough. So many others have suffered at the hands of this unknown killer. That is why we decided, as many as wished, to take refuge in the Enchanted Glade. At least we are safe here.'

'But what about Oswain? Where is he?' Sarah asked.

'That is a real mystery,' Trotter answered. 'No one has seen him now for many a moon and I am deeply concerned for his safety.' He sighed wearily. 'I don't know the whereabouts of Peter and Andrew either. We must trust Elmesh. We are here in the Enchanted Glade. It is the one place where we might obtain some answers.'

Sarah sniffed. 'I'm sorry,' she said. 'It wasn't fair of me to go on at you like that. I was being very selfish – just thinking about my own happiness and never thinking about what you and everyone else are going through.'

Trotter patted her hand. 'It's all right, Sarah,' he said. 'I am slowly getting over my loss – though I shall always miss her. It's the present troubles that concern me. And I am glad that you have come,' he added with a smile.

'You must be terribly worried,' Sarah replied. 'What I don't understand is why it has all happened. I thought the Merestone was supposed to protect the Great Forest. Or has that gone too?'

'No, it is still beside the Star Pool. Ever since Oswain returned it to its rightful place it has faithfully brought life and happiness to the forest.' He paused. 'But you must understand that if folk no longer appreciate it, then its power is diminished. Who knows what evils might be let loose if folk put their trust in themselves instead?'

William coughed. 'Excuse me, sir,' he said, addressing Trotter. 'I'm only a simple hedgehog, and I'm sorry of course to hear your news, but would I be right in thinking that's what has happened where Taril and I come from? You see, apart from the members of our Guild, everyone else seems to doubt the old wisdom. Why, some even say the stories never happened – and worse.'

Trotter nodded. 'Such is the menace that even now presses in upon us. Doubt and mistrust are part of the evil that is being sown in the hearts of the forest-folk.'

Sarah shuddered at his words. Loyalty among the forest-folk had been their strength in times past. What would happen if they now betrayed each other?

Taril spoke up. 'If only King Oswain were here,' he said. 'Surely he could unite the people.'

'Indeed he could,' agreed Trotter. 'But we really do not know what has become of him.'

Prompted by their questions, Trotter explained how three summers ago Oswain had set out alone on his horse, Firewind. He went to investigate rumours that there was trouble on the Waste Plains to the west of the forest. Travellers told of underground rumbles and earth tremors. They also spoke of bands of thieves roaming the countryside and some claimed to have lost all their possessions while they slept.

The plan was for Oswain to take a look and then ride on to the city of Elmar, where he could discuss matters with his father, the High King Argil, and his advisers. Together they would decide what necessary action to take.

'He never arrived,' said Trotter. 'When we heard nothing, we sent messengers to Elmar. The alarm was raised and a search party sent out, but they found no trace, not even of Firewind's hoof-marks. When the news reached us here, Loriana herself set off to seek him.' He shook his head sorrowfully. 'From time to time we hear that she is still searching, but, alas, to no avail.'

He heaved a great sigh.

'To make matters worse, raiders are troubling the Kingdom of Traun, so much so that King Surin is fully occupied in dealing with the problem. Then only last week I received news that there is unrest in Elmar as well.'

'Then the troubles we have in the South are part of something greater?' ventured Taril.

'Indeed they are,' replied the badger. 'These events are going to affect every one of us.'

'Did you mean it when you said that it marks the end of the world?' asked William.

Trotter rose shakily to his feet.

'It is not I who say it. I will show you,' he answered. 'Come with me.'

As Trotter led the little party deeper into the glade, Sarah grew increasingly glum. She didn't much fancy the idea of the end of the world, but there seemed little she could do about it. It was obvious too that Trotter was now too old to take charge of the forest. She felt very alone and quite helpless.

Trotter led them through the muted shadows to a crag that jutted from a grassy slope in the ground. There he fished around in a small alcove in the rock. Slowly and reverently he drew out an old book with a worn leather cover.

'I've seen that before,' exclaimed Sarah. 'Isn't it the book we found in Tergan's lair? I've forgotten what it's called though.'

'It is the same book,' Trotter acknowledged. 'And it is

called *The Tale of the Seven Rainbows*. It is the Book of Truth. You should not forget its name, Sarah.'

He laid the book on the ground and slowly opened it. Carefully he turned the pages. The ancient parchment glowed with a rainbow haze so that they needed no other light by which to read. A strange script covered the pages. Sarah could not understand any of the words, though she seemed to recall that when they first uncovered the book in the ruin of the Island of Aethius, her brother, Peter, had at least been able to read the words.* She said as much and Trotter explained that it had proved to be a very odd book. At different times only some parts made sense, but later on those parts might make no sense at all and then something else would become readable.

Page after page passed before their eyes as Trotter turned them. Then suddenly Sarah stopped him.

'Look!' she cried. 'There's a bit I can read.'

'Ah,' acknowledged the badger. 'So there is. Read it out loud, my dear.'

Sarah read: 'This is the sign of the last day. Dawn will break at midnight, and the end is only the beginning. Dark troubles will swirl like cloudy water, yet from their gloom shall burst fresh light. When fear-shrouded doubters least expect it, new things will spring from the old. Courage! All shall be mended at the coming of the King.'

They pondered the words together.

---

*You can read all about this in *Oswain and the Secret of the Lost Island*.

'Now you understand what I mean,' said Trotter, breaking the silence. 'We are on the brink of great events. A new world is coming when everything will change for the better. But first we must face those dark troubles.'

Sarah felt stirred by the words. 'Yes, I can see all that. I think I understand what you mean,' she said. 'But surely we must do something. We can't just sit here waiting for whatever it is to happen, can we? I mean, there's danger in the forest and Oswain's in some kind of trouble. We've just got to find him. If he's the King then surely we're supposed to be ready for him.'

Trotter sighed. 'You are right of course, Sarah. To tell you the truth, I am feeling my age. The loss of Oswain and then of my wife has been grievous and so I do sit here watching and waiting. There is little more that I am capable of.' He gave her a wan smile and shrugged with resignation.

'What about the others? You say Stiggle is here. Where are the rest of them?'

'Mostly here in the glade. Fumble, Mumble, Grumble, Flip-flop – everyone who is loyal to the old ways. Yes, they are all here in the Enchanted Glade.'

'Well, it won't do to sit around,' said Sarah matter-of-factly. In spite of being up for most of the night she felt wide awake. 'Trotter, I want to take a look in the Star Pool. That's where we'll find out what's happening,' she said.

William and Taril were quite bemused by all this.

'To think that we're actually part of one of the

adventures! Who would believe it?' Taril whispered to his friend as they journeyed deeper into the Enchanted Glade.

'Yes, I know,' William replied. 'Isn't this an amazing place too? You can feel the life of Elmesh all around you. I just wonder what the pool will tell us.'

'Not long to wait now. Here it is,' said Taril. 'My, just look at that!'

They had reached a small rocky grotto that shimmered in the gloom. The air tingled with life. So much so that William felt his spines bristle and Taril felt his whiskers tremble. Set beside a small pool in the rock was a jewel of the utmost beauty, which glittered with an inner fire of its own. This was the famed Merestone.

Droplets of water fell at regular intervals from the lip of an overhanging rock, and these fed the pool. Each one, as it formed, caught the light of the star, Elrilion, and fell glowing into the pool below.

Sarah approached the Merestone. She felt a buzzing sound in her ears. It was a bit scary and she realised again the awesome power of the jewel as she drew closer to its blaze. She would not touch it. Then she gasped, peered closer and spun round to face the others.

'Trotter!' she exclaimed. 'Have you seen this? There is a shadow in the Merestone, some darkness like a scar.'

Trotter eyed her solemnly.

'So you see it too, Sarah? It bodes no good. For many days that shadow has grown and I do not know what it portends, except that I believe it grows with the doubts of the forest-folk.'

Aghast with anxiety Sarah turned at once to the Star Pool. Earnestly she gazed into the glowing water. She wished more than anything else to know about Oswain. But nothing happened. In frustration she turned aside. 'Why isn't it working?' she exclaimed.

'I think,' said Trotter gently, 'that you are trying too hard. You must trust to see, not try to see.'

Sarah let his words sink in and nodded. Slowly she raised her eyes to Elmesh's star and relaxed. Then she looked into the pool again.

At first there was still nothing to be seen. Then the water began to swirl.

Sarah saw seven golden rings lying on a blue background. Then the one furthest to the right began to tremble. Suddenly, it span into the air and fell onto the ring next to it. As it did so, the trembling ring grew in size and swallowed the ring onto which it had fallen.

The same happened to the next ring and all the while the trembling ring grew larger. This happened twice more until only three other rings remained. In a flash of insight Sarah knew at once that they represented the kingdoms of Traun and Elmar, and the Great Forest.

One of these rings grew dull. Slowly it began to crumble to dust. The trembling ring hovered over it, ready to pounce.

Sarah was appalled. The Great Forest was next in line and it would be too weak to offer any resistance at all. Before she could say anything the scene shifted and she heard a plaintive voice calling for Oswain. Loriana, the Ice Maiden, came into view. She wandered mountains and valleys, fields and villages, searching, anxiously repeating Oswain's name. Then faintly Sarah heard Oswain reply. His voice was weak and he was in pain, and Loriana could not hear him.

The water swirled again and there before her appeared the faces of her two brothers. Andrew looked scared. Peter stood on the edge of a wide grassy plain and there were horses in the distance coming towards him. Sarah tried to warn him to hide.

The next moment, the water clouded and there were no more pictures.

Very troubled, Sarah turned away. Suddenly, a great weariness overcame her. Trotter, William and Taril became blurred shapes before her eyes. She sank exhausted to the ground and fell instantly into a deep sleep.

* * *

She awoke with a jolt, to find herself surrounded by faces that were both strange and yet also familiar. It was day and the air felt really invigorating. At once she was fully awake.

'Hello, Sarah,' chorused three voices together.

'Fumble, Mumble and Grumble!' she exclaimed. 'It's you!'

Before her stood the three mice who had helped rescue Peter from the Shadow-witch's castle in a previous adventure. Once they had lived up to their names, but now they were much improved – and much older. Behind them stood Flip-flop the rabbit. Then she saw Stiggle in the background talking with his great-nephew, Taril. There were many other animals, all of whom were obviously delighted to see Sarah.

'This is more like it,' she said to herself. 'Now perhaps we can get something done about all these problems.'

She greeted all her old friends in turn. Then Trotter spoke.

'We are very glad that Elmesh has sent Sarah back to us in this time of trouble. Last night she saw very disturbing signs in the Star Pool, but then fell asleep before she could tell us,' he said. 'Perhaps she can do so now.'

Sarah addressed the small crowd and described what she had seen in the pool. 'Oswain is still alive,' she said. Everyone became very excited by this news and it took a while to regain their attention. 'I don't know how we are to find him, because I think he is a prisoner somewhere. Maybe Peter and Andrew are already helping him. Though I'm not sure,' she added doubtfully. 'Anyway, we've got to do our bit against this enemy, whoever he is. The greatest danger to the forest is that we will be divided and weakened,' she said.

'What can we do? Nobody listens to us any more,' said Flip-flop the rabbit.

Sarah thought hard. 'I think we should call a meeting to unite all the forest-folk. Trotter must speak and explain what is going on. I hope you don't mind me saying this, but it's no use hiding in this glade and feeling too old to do anything. We must act.'

At that very moment a fox came racing into the glade. He made straight for Trotter.

'You've got to come quickly,' he panted. 'There's a great delegation from the South. They want to meet with you at Aldred's Park. They say you are sheltering a criminal!'

7

Captured!

Sarah stiffened at the announcement and the other animals gasped to hear such news. Matters had sunk to a bad state when forest-folk could make such accusations against one another.

Trotter, however, was unshaken. It seemed that Sarah's determination had rekindled his old fire.

'Then we shall meet them as they request,' he stated firmly. 'It is high time we set the record straight. I may be old but they will find I am not past it when it comes to saying what is right and what is wrong!'

The badger seemed suddenly to grow in stature before Sarah's eyes.

'Follow me, everyone,' he said. 'Sarah, you will come as far as the edge of the trees by Aldred's memorial. Wait there until you are called. We don't want any unnecessary scenes.'

She nodded. This was more like the Trotter she knew and loved.

As Trotter and his band of followers drew near to Aldred's Park they could hear the tumult of many voices rising in the morning air. It was soon evident that a very large crowd had gathered. Sarah hid behind a tall elm tree and watched as the badger led the way into the clearing where Aldred's statue stood. How different things seemed from those days, she thought. The forest-folk risked their lives for one another then. Now they were full of mistrust and interested only in their own comfort.

The crowd quietened as Trotter advanced and took his place on the plinth of the statue. His presence still commanded much respect among the animals, though some who had travelled far had never seen him before.

'Good morning,' he said. 'I am delighted that you have come here to meet me, as I would find it difficult at my age to visit all of you.' A few folk chuckled at this. 'This meeting is, in any case, long overdue and it is high time we put some matters to rights,' he continued. 'For a start, I must tell you that our King, Oswain, is still alive and . . .'

'Where is he then?' cried a voice from the crowd.

'Yes, show him to us. Is he hiding?' shouted another.

Trotter waited for silence.

'We do not know all the facts yet. The Star Pool reveals only so much at a time,' he continued.

'So how can we trust it?' demanded an angry stoat from near the front of the crowd.

'We trust it because Elmesh speaks through it. That is good enough,' Trotter replied firmly.

He then told them that the biggest danger to the forest-folk was not the unknown person who stalked the paths with his deadly arrows, but their own attitudes.

'If you don't trust Elmesh, we shall be in real trouble,' he insisted. 'There is a greater enemy trying to destroy us. Whoever this shadowy hunter is, he is only a part of a much wider plot.'

'And I suppose the raiders on the Waste Plain are also only part of the plot,' shouted a sarcastic rabbit. 'How many "parts" are there going to be? That's what I want to know.'

'Hear, hear!' yelled the crowd.

'What about the girl?' demanded a large hare. He muscled his way forward until he stood in front of Trotter. 'I suppose she's completely innocent?'

'As a matter of fact, she is,' Trotter replied, undaunted by the challenge. 'She is no less a person than Sarah Brown, of whom many of you have heard. She is on our side.'

A buzz ran through the crowd at this news.

'I don't believe you,' retorted the hare. He turned to the crowd and waved his paws angrily. 'Now see here,' he cried. 'You may want to believe this old badger and his talk of the Star Pool, but I for one don't. As far as I am concerned, he and his ancient followers are out of touch with the real world. They shelter in this Enchanted Glade of theirs and think we should all leave our homes to join them. Well, it won't do. We have lives to live and we can't do it by waiting for half-answers from the Star Pool. We must organise ourselves for our own protection. The future lies in the republic, not in some old fool tales.'

The crowd roared their approval and Sarah, still hidden behind the elm, feared for Trotter and his friends. Things were becoming ugly.

'We know you've got the girl with you, so hand her over,' demanded the hare.

'I will do nothing of the sort,' Trotter answered stoutly. 'Now listen here, you young upstart, you don't know what you are talking about. You have no idea of the forces being unleashed. Let me tell you, the end of the world draws near and you are not in the least prepared for it.'

The hare scoffed at this and a large number of other hares came forward to join him. Trotter's little band was greatly outnumbered.

'Your advice is not needed, old badger,' said the hare. 'You can live out your days with your friends in the Enchanted Glade if you wish, but in the King's absence we have sought other advisers.'

Trotter stiffened visibly at this news.

'What do you mean . . .' he began.

Out of the corner of her eye Sarah saw a movement. It was the shadowy figure of a man, but he was well camouflaged. The next instant, she heard a faint hiss. It was followed by a terrible wail of pain and despair. To her horror and that of everyone else gathered by the memorial, a rabbit fell stricken to the ground. A fierce arrow stuck from his body.

Pandemonium was let loose. Forest-folk screamed and screeched as they sought cover in the undergrowth. Some bolted for their lives. Only the fearless Trotter stood his ground, but his face was etched with grief and he looked very old indeed.

Sarah was just about to throw caution to the wind and

run to join him when suddenly she was seized in a vicious grip from behind.

'Got you! Got you at last!' snarled a cruel voice.

Sarah screamed with fear.

The next instant, the strong hands that pinioned her arms propelled her forward into the open. Trotter looked aghast as he saw what was happening.

'It's all right, everyone, you can come out now. The enemy is captured,' cried the voice of the one who held her.

Slowly and cautiously, the forest-folk began to re-appear. Sarah struggled in vain against the grip of her captor. Somehow his voice seemed vaguely familiar, but she couldn't quite place it.

'Here is your murderer,' snapped her captor to the reassembled mob.

'Yes,' said another voice, this one silky smooth. 'We have her weapons right here.'

He stepped forward holding a bow and several arrows. Sarah started in horror the moment she saw his short round figure and bald head. 'Sorda!' she gasped. She realised then that it must be none other than the wizard, Terras, who held her fast.

'It's not true!' she screamed. 'These men are liars. They are terrible enemies of the forest-folk. You mustn't believe them. They tried to kill me once before.'

'What she says is true,' said Trotter. 'These two men were long ago banished from the Great Forest because of their crimes.'

The hare stepped forward.

'These are our new advisers,' he stated. 'We have no cause to doubt their wisdom. They are helping us set up the republic.' He turned accusingly on Trotter and his hapless band of companions. The dead rabbit lay before them. 'A terrible murder has been committed before our very eyes this morning. You have done nothing to prevent it, nor any of the other deaths of recent months. Indeed, you have sheltered the criminal. You are under arrest, every one of you. Guards!'

The crowd roared their approval. At once, the hares seized Trotter and his friends.

'Take them back to the Enchanted Glade and set a guard at the entrance. They are to be confined there until we can set up a proper court. As for the girl, she will come with us. We will deal with her straight away!'

'No, no! You are making a terrible mistake,' Trotter insisted. But his pleas went unheard as they led him away.

Sarah was shattered beyond belief by the turn of events. Powerless to struggle or even to cry out, she was marched away.

'Got you at last,' gloated Terras's voice in her ear. 'And this time there will be no mistake!'

* * *

Peter woke with a yawn and then blinked in the bright morning light that streamed through the trees. For a moment he imagined he must be somewhere in the Great Forest. Then the events of the previous day came flooding back.

In an instant he was wide awake. He had to find Andrew.

'You slept like a log,' said a voice from the nearest tree trunk. The sound startled Peter until he remembered the Barkums.

In the daylight they were almost invisible and only by concentrating could he make out the faint glow of their eyes and their figures against the tree trunks. They appeared to be able to change their shape and colour to suit their background, like chameleons.

He smiled. At least here were some friendly creatures who might help him.

'I've got to find my brother. You will help me, won't you?' he said.

'Our sap is rising to the challenge!' exclaimed Oakum. 'If it's within our power, we'll do it.'

'We are very angry with this Feldrog and his giants,' said Alderum. 'While you slept Pineum told us of the destruction of yet more trees. He was really needled and it was all I could do to stop him chasing straight after them.'

'That kind of hasty action is typical of young Pineum,' said Oakum. 'They would crush him to pulp. No, what we need is stealth.'

'Can you get me to the Etins' camp? Maybe then we can think of a plan,' ventured Peter.

'We can, but even these woods are dangerous.

Everything is dangerous. We risk life and limb remaining here, but it is our home,' said Sycum.

'The real danger comes when we have to leave the shelter of the trees and cross the open grassland,' said Birchum. 'By my bark, I don't find that very appealing!'

After much discussion, the Barkums decided they would go as far as the eastern edge of the woods and then decide what to do. At the first sign of trouble they would hide Peter against a tree by standing in front of him.

All that morning Peter followed the flitting forms of his strange companions through the woodlands. The Barkums chattered away to each other with their woody voices, all the time making their awful puns, like when Pineum pretended to chat up the attractive Hazelum.

'I'm pining for you, darling,' he sighed.

'Oh, leaf off, will yew!'

'Can't I try to bole a maiden over?'

'Why don't you go berry your head?'

'I'm nuts over you!'

'Completely conkers, if you ask me!'

Pineum sighed. 'You've got me stumped, that's for sure.'

'Well, stop giving me the pip, then.'

'Oh, cherry-o, then!'

With the sun filtering pleasantly through the trees onto the leafy paths, Peter could almost forget the dangers and the plight of his brother.

Suddenly Oakum whirled round and hissed, 'Danger ahead! Take cover.'

The Barkums pushed Peter smartly against the nearest tree and quickly surrounded him. Their forms completely blotted out the light so that he could see nothing at all. He hoped that he was just as invisible to anyone looking for him.

Presently he heard low guttural voices.

'Search high and low, that was the Master's command. Find the other one.'

'What are we looking for?'

'How should I know, idiot? We just have to look for anything unusual that moves and capture it. The Master will decide if it's what he's after.'

'Supposing it isn't?'

'Then we'll have to keep on looking, won't we? Pity about the beating you'll get though!'

'Why me?'

'Because you're the junior, that's why. So keep your eyes peeled.'

The voices faded into the distance and Peter breathed again. So they knew he was out here, somehow. He wondered how they had obtained the information. Feldrog must have captured Andrew and made him talk. It was not a pleasant thought.

The Barkums removed themselves from him. They were delighted with their success.

'That had them barking up the wrong tree, didn't it?' chortled Alderum.

'They never twigged a thing,' agreed Birchum.

There were no further incidents and by lunchtime the party had reached the perimeter of the woods. To their left in the distance Peter could make out the causeway, though it was hazy in the bright sunshine. Ahead stretched a wide grassy plain that really offered no cover at all.

'You will have to cross this and then turn north to reach Feldrog's camp,' explained Oakum. 'It's too dangerous to go closer to the road.'

'We can't let Peter cross this moorland without help, though,' said Sycum.

'True,' Oakum acknowledged. 'But who will go with him?'

'I will,' said a voice Peter hadn't heard before. 'I'm a hardy type.'

'Laurelum!' exclaimed the others.

So after fond farewells and good wishes, Peter started out across the wide plain accompanied by the tree nymph. He felt very exposed on the rolling heath and travelled as fast as his breath would allow.

Somewhere in the distance he spied what looked to be a low ridge. There would be shelter when he got there, but he realised others might already be looking out for him. He voiced his worries to Laurelum.

'Don't worry,' replied his companion. 'I'm not afraid. Stout-hearted, they call me! If there's any trouble I'll just cover you up and we'll lie very still on the ground. Nobody will notice an old log in this long grass.'

Peter felt comforted by Laurelum's confidence and slowed his pace to a more steady walk.

After about an hour, they heard a faint rumble. At first Peter thought it was the Etins making more explosions, but this rumble didn't die away.

Then he looked ahead.

To his dismay, he could see horsemen. A whole posse was galloping towards them and the noise was the thunder of hooves. There was no time to lose. Running would be useless. He flung himself to the ground and Laurelum swiftly lay across him. Peter prayed that he would remain hidden as he heard the horses rapidly drawing nearer.

Everything might have turned out fine except for one thing. Just as the horses were passing, a hoof caught Laurelum and stumbled. It was enough for the rider to pull up and look behind him. He saw a faint movement on the grass. Not that tough old Laurelum was harmed, but he had been knocked clean off Peter and was trying to cover him again.

It was too late – the rider had spotted Peter. Wheeling his horse around he called for the others. There was nothing Peter could do except stand forlornly to his feet. In moments, a ring of fierce-looking riders had surrounded him.

To his relief, nobody took any notice of a log lying in the grass. At least Laurelum was safe.

One of the riders came forward. Like the others, he wore a short black leather tunic buckled with a studded belt. A helmet made of iron and leather protected his head. He wore a sword and carried a crossbow and a quiver full of deadly bolts. His features were Asiatic and his long black moustache reminded Peter of pictures he had seen of Ghengis Khan's warriors in his own world.

He looked down at Peter with a mocking smile.

'A runaway, by the looks of it,' he said.

His companions laughed loudly.

'But he hasn't run far enough, has he, my braves?'

This was greeted by another roar of laughter.

'Take him!' commanded the leader. 'He'll be a useful slave. Then we'll sell what's left of him back to Feldrog!'

In spite of his struggles, one of the horsemen seized Peter and threw him belly down across the saddle. The horsemen, evidently satisfied to have captured him, thundered back towards the ridge. Glumly, Peter wondered what would become of him now.

8

There Is No Escape

Slowly Peter picked himself up out of the mess of mud and straw into which he had fallen. His face was grim and he winced with pain. The sting of the horsewhip smarted across his shoulders like a hot knife. He wondered how long he could hope to survive like this at the hands of his captors.

Atag mocked him as he rose.

'Hah! By the time we finished with you I wager you be begging to go back to Feldrog! Now you work again, O worthless one. I wish all that tackle oiled by dusk or it is the worse for you, boy!'

With that Atag pushed Peter hard in the chest so that he fell back into the muck again.

'And mind it done well, or you not be fed,' he scowled as he strode off.

Peter eyed despondently the chain that linked his ankles. Several small cowbells had been attached to its length. They rattled annoyingly as he walked. Even if he managed to creep away from the Boribars' camp, the sound of the bells would give away every movement he made.

Wearily, he staggered to his feet and began work on the pile of harnesses. Since their return to the camp,

Atag had made him carry straw, fetch water, clear dung and wash pots and pans, and now he had to oil the tackle for twenty horses. Atag had beaten him every time he slowed down, and all he had eaten was an apple that he'd found on the ground.

The camp consisted of several wig-wams and a couple of covered wooden carts. In the centre a communal fire burned and the horses were tethered to posts driven into the ground. Peter soon discovered that his captors were a group of Boribar tribesmen, who were constantly on the move and lived by hunting and raiding. Judging by the way they treated him, they were a cruel race, who owed allegiance to nobody. They obviously thought Peter had escaped from Feldrog. He didn't fancy being handed over as a prisoner, that was for sure.

Atag came for him as the light was fading. To Peter's relief he seemed satisfied with the work.

'Not bad for a runaway,' he said, eyeing the pile of glistening harnesses. 'Maybe we keep you a little longer, eh?'

Peter stood silently with his head bowed. His arms ached and his hands felt raw. Suddenly a stinging blow caught him across the shoulders. He cried out in pain.

'I expect you answer when I speak to you,' Atag yelled.

Blinking back the tears of pain Peter mumbled, 'Yes sir.'

'That is better. Now you perhaps have your crust. This way.'

The Boribar led Peter towards one of the wooden

wagons. He thrust a hunk of bread and a jug of water into his hands.

'Perhaps I not tell you, you must share with the prisoner,' he sneered. 'Go on, up those steps and inside. That where you stay until morning light.'

Peter obeyed, dragging his rattling chain after him. Then with a cruel shove Atag bundled him into the darkness of the wagon and slammed the door shut. Peter heard a stout bar drop into place. It was pitch black inside the van and he had to grope around until he found a wall to rest against.

For a moment he thought his captor had been joking about another prisoner. Then he heard a faint groan.

'Hello?' he whispered tentatively.

Another groan came from the other side of the wagon.

'Where are you?' Peter asked.

'Over here,' a man croaked in reply. 'Crawl across the floor until you find me. But be careful, because I'm injured.'

Guided by the man's voice, Peter slowly felt his way across the rough wooden boards. Then he touched a booted foot and the man winced.

Soon he was alongside his fellow-prisoner.

'I've got some food and water. Not much,' he said. 'Just stale bread.'

'At least you've brought it to me,' replied the stranger. 'Usually I have to crawl around until I find it. So thank you. And have some yourself.'

Peter broke the bread and by touch put some into the man's hand. For a while they both ate and drank this miserable fare in silence.

'A feast, when there's nothing else,' said the man.

Peter agreed. 'Who are you? And why are you a prisoner?' he asked.

The man gave a short croaking laugh. 'My name is Oswain,' he said. 'I was in the wrong place at the wrong time.'

For a moment Peter couldn't believe his ears.

'Oswain!' he exclaimed. 'Oswain, the King of the Great Forest?'

'None other,' he replied ruefully.

'But Oswain, this is fantastic. It's me. I'm Peter!'

Now it was Oswain's turn to be astounded.

'Peter!' he gasped. 'I can scarcely believe it.' He reached out and grasped Peter's hand. Uncontrolled, a choking sob escaped his lips. 'I had almost given up hope,' he whispered.

Peter didn't know what to say. He had never known Oswain in weakness before and he didn't quite know how to respond. So he said nothing and just sat there in the darkness, clasping Oswain's hand. He realised there was little else he could do, for he was as much a prisoner as Oswain himself.

'I've been here a long time. It seems like for ever,' said Oswain at length. 'I've lost all track of time. They keep me in this wagon all day and all night.'

'We must find a way of escaping,' Peter answered.

Oswain gave a short laugh.

'It's not as easy as you think. I'm afraid my leg and my foot are broken,' he replied. 'They don't even bother chaining me.'

'We'll think of something,' said Peter. 'We must. We simply must.'

* * *

Andrew collapsed exhausted to the ground. About two hundred other children did the same. Some were crying.

They had toiled all day long, heaving on coarse ropes to pull Feldrog's huge chariot-throne along the newly made road. Harsh overseers had ensured that nobody slacked and those who stumbled and fell were cruelly forced back to the job.

Andrew surveyed his blistered hands. It hurt to move his fingers.

'You new here?'

Andrew glanced up at a fat boy who sat sprawled next to him. He nodded.

'Thought so. Don't worry, your hands will get used to it. I've been doing it for weeks. Look.'

He showed Andrew his callused palms.

'Tough, I am.'

'What's your name?' Andrew asked.

'Gumboil,' he replied.

'I'm Andrew.'

Gumboil shook his hand and said he would show him round. Andrew protested that all he wanted to do was sleep.

'Please yourself then,' Gumboil answered. 'But you won't get any grub – and they feed you well here.' He rose to his feet and sauntered off.

Andrew felt so exhausted that he fell at once into a deep sleep.

When he awoke it was dark. Except for the lights of the camp he could see nothing. All around him lay the sleeping forms of the other children. He lay on his back and recalled the events of the previous night. A shudder coursed through him as he thought of his first encounter with Feldrog.

The sudden disappearance and reappearance of Feldrog's camp had stunned him, but what took his breath away was the sight of Feldrog himself.

The tyrant sat high on a huge chariot-throne mounted on four wheels of gold with bright silver bosses. The chariot body was the size of a bungalow and was intricately inlaid with gold and ivory. An ornamented throne of gold was borne on the heads of four huge carved white swans. These rested in a sea consisting of millions of sparkling diamonds.

Two curving flights of red-carpeted stairs led up to the central dais on which stood the throne. On each wide step there stood a slender dancing girl clad in a long flowing skirt and a short top that left her midriff bare. From the back of the throne sprang a starburst of glittering golden spikes, each tipped with a diamond. Behind that stood a gigantic pink scalloped shell edged with gold, and sparkling with rubies, sapphires and emeralds.

Feldrog himself was a majestic black-bearded figure clad in white robes, with a scarlet sash around his middle. On his head he wore a white turban crowned with a huge ruby. He held a golden sceptre in his hand. It was long and needle-like and known as Sting.

Andrew recalled his arrogant face, and the dark piercing eyes that had struck fear into his heart. Feldrog had pointed Sting at him and the pain had been unbearable. He remembered falling to the ground and writhing in agony. Words of command had come into his heart, all of which he knew he would obey. He was not hypnotised. It was fear of Sting, and the wrath of Feldrog, that held him rooted to the spot. Nameless dreads seemed to surround him and threaten that even one step out of line would bring him to a fate worse than death. Like a lamb Andrew had knelt before the mighty potentate.

All the world would bow the knee to Feldrog the Supreme. No one could avoid it. He was the King of all kings. Andrew did not deserve to live, but as a concession he would be spared and granted the privilege of pulling Feldrog's throne. For this high honour he would be fed until it pleased Feldrog otherwise.

Meekly, Andrew had obeyed. As soon as it was light he joined with the other children in pulling the ten white ropes attached to the front of the chariot. He saw that following the chariot were armies so vast that he could not see the end of the column.

By the close of the day the chariot had reached the edge of the Bandymarsh. Andrew wondered what had happened to Peter. They had not passed his body on the road, so he assumed that he must still be alive. Perhaps Peter would somehow rescue him. However, the moment such thoughts came into his mind he felt a sudden chill of fear. Feldrog and those invisible dreads would not allow him to escape easily.

'Keep away from here, Pete,' he had thought. 'Whatever you do, keep away!'

Now he felt hungry. Staggering to his feet he eased the stiffness from his joints. Then, stepping gingerly over the sleeping forms of the other children, he tried to find some food.

Eventually he came across a row of trestle tables upon which he could make out the remnants of a meal. And there he found Gumboil.

'Oh, there you are. You're lucky to find anything left,' he said through a mouthful of food.

Andrew gave him a weak smile and began to help himself to scraps of cheese and bread and meat. He could see no sign of any guards and mentioned the fact to Gumboil.

'Oh well, they aren't needed,' said his companion. 'I mean, I don't know about you but I'd be too terrified to run away. It's them. You know – the dreads, and Sting of course. Besides, they feed you all right.'

'Has anyone ever escaped?' Andrew asked.

'Oh, every so often someone does it, but they always come back. They get caught or they have an accident. No one can escape Feldrog, that's for sure.'

'What do you know about him? He seems incredibly powerful and wealthy,' said Andrew.

Gumboil shrugged. 'I reckon he's going to take over the world. Simple as that. Best to be on his side, that's what I say. If we keep out of trouble maybe we'll get a reward of some kind when it's all done.'

Andrew asked where Gumboil had come from and he discovered that he was from a town called Esterness. Feldrog had captured it and left a company of troops to keep the people in order. Wherever he conquered, he destroyed all the leading people. Then he took some of the children captive to replace those who had fallen by the wayside pulling his chariot.

'So where's he going to stop?' Andrew wanted to know.

Gumboil shrugged. 'When he's reached the Western Sea, I suppose. Who knows? I don't care anyway.' He stuffed some bread into his mouth.

Andrew eyed him closely. 'What happened to your family, Gumboil?' he said slowly.

'Feldrog's men killed them all,' he said. 'I don't want to talk about it. Leave me alone. Go on! Leave me alone.'

Andrew left him and wandered back to his place among the sleeping children. He tried to think. Somehow Feldrog had to be stopped. But as soon as the thought came into his mind so did the horrible fear, and he felt completely weak and useless. With a sigh he settled down to sleep.

* * *

Sarah stood staring through the bars of her prison cell. It could well be the last night of her life. That afternoon the hares had tried her and found her guilty of the murder of the rabbit. They had also decided that she was most likely the person who had killed many other forest-folk.

In spite of her protests of innocence and her pleas for the forest-folk not to believe the lies of Terras and Sorda, they had found her guilty and sentenced her to be hung the next day.

Weeping, she was escorted away, tied with coarse ropes and dumped in the guard-house. She could still see in her mind's eye the gloating faces of Terras and Sorda as they mocked her plight.

Outside all was still. She could make out the shadowy shapes of the hares who stood guard around the prison. They were going to make sure she didn't escape, that was for sure. Beyond them lay the trees, but that wasn't what took her eye. Instead she focused on the gaunt outline of the hangman's gallows that was to be her fate at the first light of dawn.

There were no stars in the sky to comfort her. Elrilion was nowhere to be seen.

'Is this how it's all to end?' she pondered. Sarah didn't feel afraid of death. Just sad. What would become of the Great Forest and all her friends? Where were Oswain and Loriana? Would Terras and Sorda become the new rulers of this so-called republic?

Suddenly her thoughts were interrupted. She could hear a very faint scraping noise somewhere near her feet. Stooping down she peered into the gloom and dimly she could see a movement on the ground. Hardly daring to breathe she looked closer.

The next moment, a small furry nose poked out of the ground and a mouse's voice squeaked at her.

'Hello, Sarah – it's me. Fumble!'

9

A Daring Plan

'Fumble!' Sarah gasped. 'How did you manage to get in here?'

Before the mouse could reply, another furry head popped out of the ground.

'Guess who? It's me – Grumble,' piped the second mouse. Mumble followed very quickly behind.

'Aha,' said Fumble, once they were all assembled. He touched his nose and gave Sarah a knowing smile. 'Do you remember long ago when we met Hagbane in this clearing? We dug lots of tunnels so that we could beat a hasty retreat if we needed to.'

'Well, most of them have long since caved in,' said Mumble, taking up the story. 'But we found one that hadn't and it came up more or less underneath this hut. We only had to do a little bit of digging to reach you.'

Sarah stooped down as far as her bonds would allow. 'It's really good to see you and it's very brave of you to come like this,' she said. 'But what can you do to help me? I can't really get down that little tunnel, can I?'

'We've got a cunning plan,' said Grumble. 'First, we're going to gnaw most of the way through your ropes so that they'll snap easily when the time is ripe. Then we've arranged one or two surprises to help you get back to the Enchanted Glade.'

Between them the three mice explained the rest of their plan and then departed the way they had come. The guards never stirred. Eventually Sarah drifted off into a fitful sleep.

Many points of light floated before her eyes. One by one they went out until only three remained. The darkness grew. She heard horrible rasping sounds, and hollow laughter echoed through her mind. Nameless shapes curled around her feet. It was all she could do not to lose her nerve and start screaming. She fixed her eyes steadfastly on the remaining points of light. One of them was flickering. She knew it stood for the Great Forest. It mustn't go out. She willed it to remain strong.

The air grew chill and she woke shivering to find that it was already day. A hare was shaking her roughly.

'The prisoner will be escorted to the place of execution,' he said in a flat voice.

They would not even allow Sarah to walk. Two other guards entered the hut and between them they hoisted her onto their shoulders and carried her outside. Sarah was careful not to struggle in case her bonds accidentally snapped and gave the game away.

She blinked in the bright sunshine on what was intended to be the last morning of her life and thought how beautiful the world was. Many people must die on sunny mornings. It made her sorrowful to think about it.

Terras and Sorda were standing by the gaunt gallows. Terras, the taller of the pair, sneered as the hares approached with their living burden. Sorda wore his usual oily smile. His bald head shone in the sunlight.

A crowd of forest-folk had gathered for the spectacle. There were a large number of hares, and Sarah suspected that most of the others were those who had had relatives murdered by the sinister archer. She felt quite sure that in normal times forest-folk would never attend a public execution!

She searched the crowd for any of her friends but could see nobody she knew.

The hares dragged her up the wooden steps and onto the platform of the gallows. It housed a simple trapdoor operated by a big wooden lever. Terras stood beside it. He would be the executioner. The menacing noose hung before Sarah's eyes. She could feel her heart beating faster. What if the plan misfired? She was only minutes from death.

'Welcome to the Republic of Alamore. Heavenly morning for a hanging, isn't it? Hm, perhaps we should call it the republic of heaven,' Terras mocked. 'Though in your case it's more like the republic of hell!'

With a great effort of will, Sarah kept her mouth shut. There was a lot she would have liked to say!

Sorda chuckled as he reached up and put the noose over her head. He pulled it tight and she could feel the coarseness of the rope scratching her neck. She winced and twisted uncomfortably.

Then one of the hares, whom Sarah recognised to be the chief judge who had tried her the day before, stood before the crowd. He read from a scroll in a formal, grave voice.

'The girl, Sarah Brown, first arrested under suspicious circumstances, having escaped, did then continue to terrorise the Great Forest. She, being caught red-handed with the weapon that killed one Simon Rabbit, was then taken into custody. Having been duly tried by the people's court and found guilty of murder, she has been sentenced to death. In the name of the republic this sentence is now legally authorised to be carried out.'

Sarah stood stock still. Her heart was thumping. Already the rope seemed to be strangling her and her mouth felt dry. She wanted to scream out that it was all a terrible mistake. Perhaps it was a bad dream and she would wake at any moment. Her whole short life seemed to pass before her eyes – places she had been, her parents and her brothers, her school friends, her bedroom and her toys.

Terras had his hand on the lever and she could see his knuckles whiten as he grasped it. The air hung with a tense silence and not a person moved in the watching crowd.

'Farewell, and here's to hell, child!' he smirked.

He thrust the lever down hard. The trapdoor sprang open and Sarah dropped like a stone. The noose jerked tight around her neck.

The next moment, she hit the ground. The rope had mercifully snapped, nine-tenths having been eaten through by Mumble during the night. Sarah wrestled with her bonds. These too broke like flax. Desperately, she clawed at the noose around her neck and pulled it free. She gulped in a great gasp of air.

But there was no time to lose. She had the element of surprise on her side and she had to use it at once.

Before the astounded onlookers could recover their wits, she sprang from beneath the gallows and ran for all she was worth straight at the crowd that barred the direction between her and the Enchanted Glade. She was so desperate that she scattered them aside like pins in a bowling alley.

However, her captors were quick to recover.

'After her!' screamed Sorda. 'Don't let the prisoner escape!'

'Strike her down!' yelled Terras. He was white with fury.

The fleet-footed hares at once muscled through the confused crowd and gave chase.

Sarah ran for her life. She knew for sure that her head start would not last long against the speed of her pursuers. Indeed a swift glance across her shoulder revealed that they were already much closer than she would have liked. She redoubled her efforts and sprinted for the path that led to the Enchanted Glade.

The leading hares were closing fast. She would never make it. At any moment she would feel their paws wrap around her legs and bring her crashing to the ground. The nearest one was almost at her ankles.

Suddenly, she heard a shriek of frustration. Glancing over her shoulder, she saw that a cunningly **hidden** net had sprung up across the path immediately **behind** her and in front of her pursuers. They had careered straight into it and become thoroughly entangled in the mesh.

'Good old Fumble, Mumble and Grumble!' she gasped to herself as she fled towards the glade.

At last she saw the sentinel stones just ahead of her through the trees. Panting with relief she stumbled towards them. However, it was not over yet. Three of the hares had freed themselves from the net and were again at her heels. It would be touch and go if she made it in time, and even then what could she do once she was within the glade? They would surely follow her.

Just when all seemed lost and the hares looked like catching her after all, she heard a commotion behind her. She looked round to see the three hares screeching and struggling on the ground. The cause of their discomfort was immediately apparent. Several large hedgehogs, rolled up in balls, had dropped from the branches of an overhanging tree straight into the hares' path. Sarah's pursuers were writhing in pain as the hedgehogs bounced all over them and spiked them with their quills.

The hedgehogs didn't hang about, however. As soon as they saw that Sarah was in the clear they themselves lost no time in scampering towards the Enchanted Glade as fast as their short legs could carry them. Sarah saw that one of them was William. His eyes were bright with excitement.

'Just think,' he puffed. 'I've taken part in one of your adventures! There's one for the Guild!'

Sarah laughed as she looked back at the hares. They were licking their wounds and looking very sorry for themselves.

'And a very important part too. That's the second time you've helped me. Are these friends of yours?' she panted as the other hedgehogs joined them.

'Yes,' he said proudly. 'We're all members of the Guild. You see . . .'

'Tell me more about them later,' Sarah interrupted. 'We're still not out of danger. They'll be after us again in a moment.'

'I don't think so,' came a familiar voice from the glade.

Sarah looked round to see Trotter standing just beyond the sentinel stones.

'Come on,' he said. 'You'll be safe here.'

Sarah and the hedgehogs gained the sanctuary of the Enchanted Glade just as the rest of the hares sped into view. She wondered why Trotter was so calm. He was smiling to himself and humming lightly.

She soon discovered the reason. The hares, with their eyes fixed on the quarry, hurtled heedlessly between the sentinel stones. And there they came to an abrupt and extremely uncomfortable halt. It was just as though someone had fixed an invisible plate of unbreakable glass across the entrance. Try as they might, the bruised and battered hares could go no further.

Sarah asked Trotter for an explanation.

'It's simple,' he said, eyeing the frustrated efforts of the hares. 'When they arrested you and sought to have you put to death, they committed an act of appalling injustice. As a result, Elmesh has banned them from the Enchanted Glade, even though they are forest-folk. Only the true-hearted will be able to enter from now on, and most of them are already here. Those who are false, all those who follow those liars, Terras and Sorda, will be kept outside. Now come, my dear,' he said with a satisfied smile. 'Help me with my poor old tottering legs, will you? It's time you had some breakfast.'

10

Prisoners of the Boribars

Oswain and Peter spoke long into the night.

'I was out on the Waste Plains to the east of the Great Forest, checking rumours that brigands were roaming the countryside,' he began. 'We had received stories of travellers being attacked and robbed of all they possessed. It was part of the unrest felt in all our kingdoms.'

'I remember those Waste Plains,' said Peter. 'That was where we once had a very narrow escape.'

'Oh yes,' said Oswain with feeling. 'Well, that wasn't the end of the story, as I was soon to find out. At the time, I was talking to my horse, Firewind. He had picked up the scent of other horses on the breeze. We began to follow his nose and it led us to the other side of the Waste Plains and up onto the old ridge. That's where it all happened.'

He shifted his position on the floor and winced as he did so.

'All of a sudden, there was a terrible upheaval in the ground. Everything became confused. I remember hearing Firewind whinny in alarm, and the next moment I was thrown to the ground. Firewind fell too, and I could see him just about to struggle to his feet when a huge spout of mud shot into the air and crashed down onto him. The sheer weight of it trapped him. Before I could do anything to help, a rock struck my leg and broke it.'

Peter flinched at the thought.

'That must have really hurt,' he said.

'It was agony,' Oswain answered ruefully.

'The Earth-Trog?' Peter suggested.

'You've guessed it in one. Yes, it was the Earth-Trog. I could hear his voice. "Revenge! Revenge!" he cried. "Now you will die." '

'So then what happened?' Peter asked.

'Those horses Firewind had scented belonged to the brigands, the Boribars. They came on the scene just at that moment. In a way I suppose I owe them my life. Somehow the Earth-Trog seemed to recognise his own kind, for the ground settled down and the Boribars took me prisoner. They bargained with the Earth-Trog that they would take me to someone called Feldrog. In return, he would be rewarded with many children to devour.'

'Ugh! What happened to Firewind?' Peter asked.

'Oh, they dug him out of the mud and took him in tow too.'

Peter wanted to know what happened next.

'I can't tell you,' Oswain replied. 'They were so rough with me, what with my broken leg and the bruises from the fall, that I must have lost consciousness. By the time I came round I was locked in this wagon.

'They were obviously in no hurry to hand me over,' Oswain continued. 'They set my leg for me – very roughly, I might add, and then once it had healed they treated me as their slave while they continued their raids on people's farms. That was two years ago and more.'

'So you've been away from the Great Forest for all that time?' Peter asked. 'And nobody's come to rescue you?'

'I am sure they tried once they realised that I was missing, but the Boribars travelled far to the south to skirt the Great Forest. Then they crossed the mountains eastwards by tracks that few would know. Why should anyone have suspected that I was their captive, let alone where I was?'

Peter nodded his head in the dark. One matter still puzzled him. 'When they threw me in here with you, you said you were injured. What's wrong?' he asked.

Oswain gave a rueful laugh. 'I tried to escape – on more than one occasion, as you would expect – but they kept me weighed down with chains and bells. In the end, Atag, their leader, had had enough of me so he decided to fit an iron ball to my leg chains. Then, just to make sure, Atag dropped the ball on my foot and broke the bones, after which he broke my shinbone.'

'The filthy rat!' Peter exclaimed.

'Of course, I couldn't work after that,' Oswain continued. 'So they removed my chains and locked me up in this wagon more or less day and night, and that's where I've been ever since. I don't know how long I've been here, or where we are. It's like being in limbo.'

Now Peter understood why Oswain had been so near to despair. His own problems seemed very small compared to what Oswain had suffered. He was also deeply angry over the Boribars' cruelty.

'So how on earth did you become a prisoner of the Boribars?' Oswain asked. 'You are the last person I ever expected to meet in this cell!'

Peter gave a short laugh.

'I didn't expect to be here either,' he answered. 'It all began like this. . . .'

Peter recounted how he and Andrew had arrived in the Bandymarsh and discovered the Glumps and their problems. He then explained how they had come across the Etins and the road they were building, and what he and Andrew had overheard about Feldrog.

At this, Oswain grew restless.

'This is grave news indeed,' he said. 'Trouble has been brewing in the East for a long time and we received rumours about a tyrant who wanted to conquer the world. Evidently it is Feldrog and he is now on the move with his armies. That's the only reason for build-ing such a road.' He grasped Peter's arm. 'He's got to be stopped somehow. The Great Forest, Surin's realm, and Elmar itself are in terrible danger. You must escape and warn them, Peter.'

'But even if I find a way of escaping, I can't leave you here,' Peter protested.

'My fate isn't important, and my guess is that my friends and family are spending all their energies seek-ing me. They must stop that and prepare to face this ruthless foe.'

Peter shifted uncomfortably on the floor.

'I'll find a way somehow,' he said. 'But I'm not leav-ing you behind.'

'Find Firewind. He'll be with the other horses. He can talk, of course. That's how you'll know who he is. Now you'd better get some sleep while you can.'

* * *

The Boribars were evidently in no hurry to move and for the next two days Peter was not only kept busy but was constantly under the watchful eye of Atag. Each evening, when he was thrown back into the wagon with Oswain, he carried only the glum news that he had not been allowed near the horses.

On the same morning that Sarah had faced her execution in the Great Forest, Peter found himself as busy as ever with the many chores of the Boribars' camp, but today Atag left him to get on with things by himself. Not only were there pots and pans to be scrubbed and water to be fetched, but he was told to feed the horses. At last he had his opportunity.

'Which one of you is Firewind?' he hissed as he opened a sack of oats. There was no reply. All he got were the snorts and quiet whinnyings of the horses as they nosed into the food.

Peter asked again, but there was no sign that any of the horses recognised the name or could speak. Oswain must have got it wrong, he concluded glumly. Either Firewind was dead, or he had been sold.

Clanking his chain he returned to the camp fire where

the Boribars were finishing their breakfast.

'Hey, come here, wretch,' laughed one of the men. 'You eaten yet?'

Peter shook his head.

'Have this then,' laughed the man. He threw Peter a bone that he had been chewing on. It fell at Peter's feet, and all the men roared with laughter.

When Peter refused to pick it up, Atag rose and took him roughly by the scruff of the neck. He forced the boy to his knees and made him gnaw at the bone like a dog, much to the amusement of his fellow-brigands.

'Leave him, Atag,' said one of them after a while. 'There's work needs doing and we move on to meet Feldrog today, don't forget.'

Reluctantly, Atag let him go.

Peter's chance came as he was lugging the large cooking pots over to the other wooden wagon. There, to his surprise, he came across a solitary horse harnessed between the shafts. He saw that it was muzzled with a broad leather band.

Glancing behind him to ensure that the coast was clear, Peter approached as quietly as he could.

'Are you Firewind?' he hissed. 'Nod three times if you are.'

To his delight the horse nodded. Quickly, Peter explained that he was a friend of Oswain's. He had to escape and warn everyone about the terrible danger facing the Great Forest. He asked if the horse would help him.

The horse nodded again.

'I'll be back,' said Peter. 'First I've got to find a way of removing this chain.'

He slipped away behind the wagon and began to heave the pots and pans noisily up its steps.

Inside he saw what he was looking for. Lying all around were a blacksmith's tools and equipment. Peter spotted a hammer and chisel.

'Just what I need,' he breathed. Then, taking his chance, he struck the chain over an anvil. It took several blows to sever it. Peter was careful to intersperse these with clattering the pots and pans so that the noise didn't sound too obvious. He then set to work on the other end of the chain.

Just as he was starting to feel pleased with himself, he heard Atag's voice from across the field.

'Boy, where are you? Come here! I want you work here, now!'

Peter spied through a crack in the wall. Atag was coming in his direction. In panic, he glanced at the tell-tale chain, wondering what he could do. Then he spotted some short lengths of rawhide. Swiftly, he tied the chain back together and hoped that Atag would not look closely.

He was only just in time.

'Coming, sir. I was busy in here putting things to rights,' he said as Atag's scowling face appeared. The Boribar glanced around suspiciously, but to Peter's relief said nothing.

'Get horses harnessed up, and quick about it,' he growled.

Peter realised that he would have to bide his time and wait for the right opportunity to make his escape. For the rest of the morning he had to content himself with sitting on the wagon drawn by Firewind as the Boribars made their way north towards the highway.

By noon they were almost there, and Peter's spirits were beginning to droop. The closer they got to Feldrog, the greater he felt his chances were of being caught.

Amid much shouting and swearing, the horses and the wagons were manoeuvred onto the road during the early afternoon. The Boribars judged from the marks left on the road that Feldrog's entourage had already passed. They would have to travel west to catch up.

All afternoon the company rattled along the road. Their wagons limited their speed and, much to Peter's relief, they had still not caught sight of Feldrog's men by the time the sun was sinking low in the sky. The air grew cool and Peter shivered. A mist began to creep across the surrounding grassland. Ahead, he could see the dark shape of woods and realised that they were close to where he had come across the Barkums. He wondered if they knew what was going on.

The mist began to thicken and soon the sun was no more than a reddish haze on the horizon.

Suddenly, one of the Boribars gave a cry. Peter looked up. Just where the causeway began to pass through the woods, someone had created a huge roadblock of felled trees. The road was quite impassable. It was a sight that made Peter's heart leap with hope.

The wagons came to a grinding halt while the

Boribars angrily surveyed the barrier.

'We must drag trees away to make path for the wagons,' said Atag. 'Just wait till I get my hands on the throat of whoever done this!'

At last Peter saw his chance. The Boribars were busy roping up the trees so that their stallions could pull them off the road.

'Do you want this one too, sir?' he called to Atag.

'Yes. Yes, and quick about it,' Atag shouted testily.

With eager fingers, Peter undid the traces and loosed the band from Firewind's muzzle. Then he undid the two pieces of rawhide holding his chain and swiftly clambered onto Firewind's back.

'Make for the trees,' he whispered. 'I've got friends there. Now, go for it!'

11

Peter Rides for Freedom

Firewind was a wise horse, descended from the steeds of Arandell who had roamed the vast plains of the early eastern world. His stock were never tamed; they chose only to serve those they thought worthy.

So instead of doing as Peter had said, Firewind backed quietly along the road until the mist closed around him and his young rider. Only then did he slip off the road and onto the open grassland.

Even then he did not gallop off as Peter expected. Instead, he padded softly across the turf in a wide arc until at length they passed under the shelter of the trees. By now, they were at some considerable distance from the road.

At some point Peter thought he could hear the muffled cries of the Boribars. They would have discovered his escape and begun searching, but the mist was thick and he and Firewind might have been anywhere. Hopefully, they thought he had made off in the opposite direction from Feldrog's camp. If so, they would probably not bother searching in the dark for long. They still had their main prize securely imprisoned in the wagon.

Although the mist was less dense in the woods, it was almost impossible to see, and Peter was grateful for

Firewind's unerring instincts as they wove between the shadowy trees.

At last Firewind came to a halt.

'What now?' asked Peter. 'Do we keep going all night or do you want to rest?'

'We should speak first to your friends,' breathed Firewind. 'They are close by and are very excited, by the feel of it.'

'Do you think they put the trees across the road?' Peter asked.

'Undeniably,' replied the horse. 'But I think they are not finished yet. We must wait and see. You may dismount if you wish.'

Two hours must have passed before Peter heard voices through the fog. By now he was cold and hungry. Sleep was beginning to overtake him but he started at the sound and was instantly alert. Firewind pricked up his ears.

'Stop horsing about and let them see you, you gnarled old fool!'

'Keep your leaves on then, and I will, O mighty oak!'

The next moment, two shadowy shapes, faintly glowing, emerged from the darkness. They looked for all the world like ragged ghosts, and Peter was glad that this was not his first meeting with the Barkums. 'Here we are,' he hissed.

'Have you twigged who we are?' said the deeper voice. 'It's me, Oakum, and Willowum is with me.'

'Well, I'm really glad you've come. I thought we'd see you earlier,' Peter replied, with a sudden shiver. The Barkums really did look like ghosts at first sight.

'Ah well, we've been busy rooting around with a few plans of our own,' Willowum answered airily, and Peter could see a knowing smile on his woody face.

'Did you block the road?' he asked. 'I thought it was you. How did you move all those trees?'

'We have our ways,' replied Oakum. He nodded sagely. 'There's not much we can't do with wood, but it wouldn't do to tell you how,' he added.

'Well, it worked and we're very grateful,' said Peter. 'You were very clever to think of it.'

'Upon my sap, it wasn't our idea!' answered Oakum. 'Firewind planned it all, don't you know?'

Peter's mouth dropped open in amazement.

'Now, your honour, would you kindly accompany us?' invited Oakum, addressing Firewind.

'Bu-bu-but . . . ' Peter stammered as Firewind nodded and began to move off. He looked at the stallion with fresh appreciation and it dawned on him that he was out of his depth in all this. Hastily he caught up with them as they disappeared into the gloom.

After about ten minutes, Peter spied a faint glow ahead. It was soon apparent that the tree nymphs had gathered in a small clearing.

'We bow in your honour,' said one as Firewind entered the clearing.

'And pleasant to see you again, Peter,' said another, whom he recognised as Birchum.

'Um, yes, hello everyone,' he replied awkwardly.

Firewind sniffed the air and then tossed his head and neighed.

'You have done well,' he said in a horsy voice.

'Indeed they have,' answered a familiar voice.

Peter could hardly believe his ears.

'Oswain!' he exclaimed. 'But how? Wh-where are you?'

The Barkums chuckled with delight at his confusion. Then two of them moved aside to reveal Oswain to Peter's astonished gaze. He was resting comfortably on a mossy couch and his left leg and foot were secured in splints.

Peter stumbled across as though he were in a dream.

'How did you escape?' he gasped. 'I just can't believe this.'

'Ah, for that you must thank the courage and cleverness of our friends – especially Laurelum,' said Oswain with a twinkle in his eye. 'He followed you to the camp, knowing nothing of my plight, of course. He simply wanted to help you escape.'

'I never saw him,' said Peter.

'Of course you did – but then you didn't,' said Laurelum, who had quietly come across to where Peter stood. 'But if you'd kept your eyes really open you might just have noticed an untidy branch that kept moving around the camp!'

Laurelum then explained that he had listened to Peter's conversation with Oswain and then spoken to Firewind.

'But he was muzzled,' said Peter. 'He couldn't talk at the time – could you, Firewind?'

'I have ways of communicating with the likes of the

Barkums that do not require my mouth to open,' replied the horse without further explanation. He ambled across and nuzzled his master.

'I came back here as fast as my twigs could carry me,' said Laurelum.

'As soon as I saw it, I thought it must be you that blocked the road,' said Peter. 'That was brilliant. I didn't realise that Firewind knew all about the plan, though. And I still don't understand how Oswain escaped.'

'It was as simple as falling off a log,' answered Oakum. 'We just opened the wagon from underneath and carried him out. I told you we have ways with wood. There's very little we can't do with it.'

'They've thought of everything,' said Oswain. 'And they make mighty good splints for broken limbs too. Here, Peter, try some of the Boribars' best food. It's time they paid you proper wages for all the work you've done! And they certainly owe me a decent meal.'

So Peter soon found himself tucking into a hearty meal thoughtfully provided by the Barkums. As he ate, they planned the next step.

'I can't be moved from here,' explained Oswain. 'You must go as fast as you can to the Great Forest and seek the help of Loriana. Firewind will assist you. Then you must warn everyone to be ready for Feldrog. Go to Elmar and advise my parents and Princess Alena. Send messages to Surin in Traun. Tell them that I am safe and that they are to prepare for a major onslaught.'

'When do I start? And what about Andrew?' asked Peter.

'You must go now, as soon as you have eaten. I cannot say what will happen to Andrew. Sometimes great sacrifices have to be made to save the lives of others.' Oswain looked on Peter's sad face. 'Cheer up! It may not be as bad as you think. Put your trust in Elmesh to make matters right. We've been in bad spots before, don't forget.'

Peter gave him a wan smile. 'Will you be all right?' he said.

'Oh, don't worry about me. The Barkums are good folk and I'll be well protected. I just wish I could ride with you,' Oswain replied.

A few minutes later Peter mounted Firewind – this time asking his permission first – and with fond farewells he was off.

To start with they moved steadily through the woods. Trees loomed out of the mist like the silent masts of ships in the night. Firewind made for higher ground. Soon the mist cleared and Peter could see the stars. Elrilion was shining brightly. He lifted his eyes and thought of Andrew. 'Please let him be all right,' he whispered. And with that he felt much better.

Firewind began to increase his pace and Peter clung tightly to the horse's powerful neck. Before long, Firewind was cantering through the light undergrowth. Then, suddenly, they broke the cover of the trees and made straight for the causeway.

'We may as well use for good what has been built for evil,' said the horse.

Once on the road, Firewind loosed his stride. Soon the

magnificent steed was flying at full gallop and Peter gasped at the speed and the unerring hooves of his mount. The wind streamed through his hair and his eyes smarted so much that he could scarcely see. Sparks flashed from Firewind's tireless hooves as he thundered along the grey ribbon of road.

Lying in muted shadows beneath the starlit sky, the countryside rolled steadily by as horse and rider hurtled through the night.

Then Peter spied a faint glow ahead in the distance.

'Feldrog,' snorted Firewind. 'Here we leave the road. Hold tight!'

With that he leapt from the causeway and onto the moorland. His pounding hooves dropped to a dull thud on the grass, but his pace did not slacken for a moment. Peter realised that they must circle round Feldrog before regaining the road. He dearly wanted to find out what had happened to his brother but knew that he must obey Oswain's orders. Firewind would not even have questioned them, he thought.

All night he rode and though he was tired the sheer energy of the mighty horse kept him wide awake. By now they were on the rising ground that led to the eastern mountains through which they would have to pass to reach the Great Forest. It seemed that Firewind had decided against returning to the road and Peter worked out that they had come to the foot of the mountains by passing behind the Bandymarsh. As far as he could determine, they could not be too far from where Feldrog's road also ran through the mountains.

Somewhere to the East, he could see a faint glow that heralded the nearness of the dawn. Firewind had slowed now as they wove through a steep narrow pass between high crags.

Suddenly, Peter saw another glow ahead. He stiffened.

'Steady, Firewind,' he breathed.

Then, from round a curve in the pass, a loud voice spoke.

'Don't move. Stay right where you are!'

* * *

Matters were bad in the Great Forest. Terras and Sorda were furious at having lost Sarah and they let their anger be felt by everyone in sight. When they tried to enter the Enchanted Glade they found it as much blocked against them as the hares. Being wizards, they tried all manner of spells, but none could break the barrier that Elmesh had erected for the safety of the faithful.

For a while Sarah and Trotter watched the spectacle, but then they moved away.

'It is very sad,' said Trotter with a sigh. 'You would think that everyone would be faithful to Oswain and to Elmesh. When I think of all we have been through . . .' He sighed again. 'But there you are, my dear. Troubled times bring out the best and the worst in all of us, and the true-hearted are revealed for who they are. No amount of loyalty when things are easy can make up for disloyalty when they are hard.'

'Can't we get any of them to change their minds?' Sarah asked.

'Maybe. Maybe,' said the badger. 'If they do they will enter the glade easily, for it tests the hearts of each and every one who approaches it. No one who is true will be barred.'

'It seems such a pity that so many are deceived,' said Sarah with a shake of her head. 'As for Terras and Sorda, how could anyone be taken in by them? They're just crooks!'

As Sarah and Trotter pondered the fate of the forest, Terras and Sorda were busy. Helped by the hares, they began to organise the animals who chose to remain outside the glade.

'You are all in danger if you stay in your houses,' Terras declared. 'We never know when this wicked girl is going to come out and attack us again. You cannot trust that old badger and his gang. Look, they have even shut themselves away by some terrible magic. If we are not careful, they will take us all prisoners.'

His henchman Sorda stood up to speak. 'We must unite ourselves in one place. It is the only way,' he said. 'There is strength in numbers. That is what the Republic of Alamore is for. Let us build a stockade where we can all be safe, and where we can defend ourselves. We will set watchmen on the walls and guard the gates day and night.'

This seemed good to the crowd, who were looking for something to do now anyway, and the hares applauded loudly. They might refuse the safety of the Enchanted Glade but they could make their own fortress instead.

'Anyone who does not enter the compound will be viewed as a traitor, an enemy to our cause,' declared Terras, and the matter was settled.

So it was that the animals began to erect a large stockade of wooden stakes in the middle of Aldred's Park. While they worked, others gathered food and built it into a great pile. Meanwhile, the word went out that all those refusing to come into the camp were to be considered enemies. As a result, animals began to stream towards Aldred's Park from all parts of the forest.

By the end of the day the project was more or less finished. A high ring of wooden stakes, secured by a strong gate and guarded by hares standing on platforms inside the wall, completed the compound. Within the camp the animals were busily organising themselves into groups for eating and sleeping. Many were finding the cramped conditions very different from what they had been used to, and a number of fights and squabbles broke out. As a result, a law was rapidly passed saying that anyone who started a fight would be banished from the camp. Only then did the quarrelling cease.

As the sun sank in the sky, the gates were closed and barred. An eerie silence fell on the Great Forest.

Inside the compound Terras and Sorda gazed at the

scene and sighed with satisfaction. They had put a sign on the gate that read: *The Republic of Alamore. Heaven on earth.*

'Good. It is good,' said Terras with a nod.

'Very good,' breathed Sorda.

12

A Welcome Meeting

Firewind halted abruptly in his tracks and Peter slipped quickly from his back. He smiled with relief at the sound of the familiar voice, though he wondered at the reason for the command.

Moments later, a shimmering cloud of spangled light began to dance above the path in front of them and a sound like the tinkling of many small fine bells filled the air. Peter suddenly felt very sleepy, and remembered that this was the effect the Naida always had on people. However, before slumber could overcome him, a slender woman materialised in the midst of the light. She wore a sapphire robe, and a silver circlet adorned her flowing hair. Instantly, Peter felt wide awake.

'Loriana!' he cried.

'Peter!' she exclaimed in reply. 'And riding no less a steed than Firewind too. This is a tale indeed. But hush, we must be careful. Our foe is not very far away and he has lookouts posted everywhere. If you had passed this bend it is likely that you would have been spotted.'

At her bidding they retreated a little down the path before speaking further.

'I'm so glad we've found you,' said Peter, still amazed. 'I mean, not that we were looking, but I did hope . . .'

The Ice Maiden interrupted him. 'The ways of Elmesh are wondrous. Far and wide I have travelled looking for Oswain. Alas, I have found no trace of him. Three days ago I felt I must come to these mountains. I arrived in the early hours of this morning and immediately spied Feldrog and his army.' Her face clouded. 'I knew then that I must end my search for my beloved and do what I could to protect the Great Forest. It was a hard choice. I rested a while and then I heard the distant sound of a horse I knew well.' She smiled at Firewind and grasped Peter's arm. Her eyes were anxious. 'Tell me now, both of you, what news of Oswain?'

Peter and Firewind told of their adventures while the Ice Maiden listened in wide-eyed amazement.

'Truly, Elmesh has caused our paths to cross,' she said slowly. 'It gives me hope in a situation of which I despaired. I did not know if Oswain was still alive.' She reached forward and kissed Peter on the cheek. 'You have given me the best news I could have hoped for. I shall not forget your courage.'

Peter was glad that the dim light of early dawn hid his flushed cheeks. 'I'd like to know what has happened to Andrew,' he said, changing the subject. 'I hope he's still alive.'

'That I cannot say,' she answered solemnly, 'except that Feldrog uses children to haul his throne. I doubt if he has killed your brother. More likely Andrew is a slave.'

'And Sarah? We haven't seen her since we arrived, so we don't know if she even came at all.'

'Of that I can give you no news,' answered the Ice Maiden. 'Maybe she is already in the Great Forest. I have been away searching for Oswain for so long that I am out of touch with events at home. Fool that I am, I should have realised that Feldrog would set his sights upon our realms.' She clenched her fists in frustration.

By this time the sun was rising, and the Naida had faded to a faint shimmer in the air. Peter asked what lay beyond the pass and what they should do next.

Loriana told him that the road had been built well up into the mountains. If he rounded the rocks, Peter would see Feldrog's camp on the floor of the valley. Simply thousands upon thousands of troops were camped with him, as well as the hundreds of slave-children who hauled his chariot-throne.

Peter bit his lip as he thought of Andrew among that number.

'Today Feldrog will reach the top of the valley and tomorrow he will be ready to invade the Great Forest,' the Ice Maiden said gravely.

'Can he not be stopped?' Peter asked. 'Just who is he, anyway?'

'I fear it may be too late for the Great Forest,' she replied sadly. 'It will take all our forces to defend the city of Elmar itself. Even so, it may not be possible. So far no kingdom has successfully resisted him.' She looked Peter in the eye. 'He comes with a terrible weapon. It is not the army that you can see, awesome though it is, but something far worse. They call it Feldrog's Sting.'

At the mention of the words Peter felt a tremor of fear pass through his body and was suddenly aware of how cold it was. 'What on earth is that?' he asked.

The Ice Maiden looked at him curiously. 'Already you feel it,' she said. 'Feldrog possesses the power to strike fear into the hearts of all who stand in his way. He does not need to speak or to threaten. He stretches forth his rod and people are simply terrified into serving him. That is how he has gathered such a vast army.' She put a comforting arm on Peter's shoulder. 'I myself am not afraid, but I do respect his power. We will not resist him easily.'

All kinds of wild imaginings filled Peter's mind. 'What does he look like? I bet he's got a really evil face. Is he human?' he asked.

The Ice Maiden shook her head. 'You would be surprised,' she said. 'He is a handsome and well-educated ruler who loves beautiful things. He is surrounded by treasures of unbelievable wealth and splendour. Yet he serves the very Darkness itself.'

Peter pondered for a few moments, then he gazed at Loriana. 'We've got to stop him, haven't we? What do you want me to do?' he asked.

The Ice Maiden smiled. 'I will go at once to my beloved and bring what healing I can,' she said. 'We will join you as soon as possible, but you must obey the King's orders. Go first to the Great Forest and speak to Trotter. He will know what action to take. Then ride on to Elmar and bid them send messages to Surin, as Oswain commanded you.'

'How will we get there? Is there another path we can take?'

Loriana shook her head. 'It will take courage once more, Peter. You will have to ride for all you are worth and hope that you can outrun Feldrog's troops and resist the power of his Sting.'

'We can do it,' said Firewind. 'I will serve my master's will and I fear nothing else, except to fail.'

Loriana stroked his muzzle affectionately.

'So we who have so soon met must now part company for a while,' she said with a sigh. 'First, though, a drink to refresh you.' So saying, she drew forth a small flask from her robe and gave both Firewind and Peter a draught. The effect was marvellous and at once they felt warmed and refreshed.

'Farewell – for now,' she said. 'Elmesh protect you until we meet again.'

Peter and Firewind watched as the Naida formed around Loriana's feet. Then, at a word of command, they lifted her off the ground and she began to journey through the air in the direction of the woods where Oswain lay waiting.

'We must go too,' breathed Firewind. 'You had better hold on tightly, for we shall run a furious race, I think.'

They emerged from the narrow pass to find themselves high up on one side of a steep grassy valley. Immediately, Peter felt the presence of evil hit him like a sudden chill gust. Firewind moved uneasily beneath him.

Down below, much activity was taking place and in

the early morning light it was obvious that already the road builders were working apace. Behind them rested Feldrog's chariot-throne in all its glittering splendour. To the rear of the royal carriage vast armies stretched in seemingly endless ranks as far as the eye could see. Peter felt mesmerised by the sight.

However, there was no time to stand and stare. With a snort from his nostrils, Firewind was off. Fleet of foot, he cantered between the rocky outcrops of the steep slope and made left towards the high saddle ridge at the head of the valley. Before many minutes he was at full gallop and Peter wondered how long they could travel at such a breakneck speed without mishap.

Not that he had any wish to slow down. The thought of Feldrog's Sting filled him with sufficient anxiety to spur him on as speedily as possible.

Suddenly, he heard a dull thud nearby. It was followed by another. A large stone bounced off one of the rocky outcrops and nearly struck them. Peter glanced back down the valley. Huge grey shapes were lumbering forward, away from the main party. With a shock he realised that he and Firewind had been spotted. The Etins were giving chase and it was they who were throwing the stones.

'Quick, Firewind!' he gasped. 'As fast as you can. They've seen us.'

Firewind said nothing. His sinews were taut as bowstrings and his lean body surged with strength as he sought to gain the ridge. Sweat sheened his chestnut coat and flecks of foam flew from his mouth.

More rocks fell around them and Peter feared that the Etins' aim was improving as they drew closer. Anxiously, he glanced back. A dozen or more of the Etins were running towards them. He peered forward again. The ridge seemed impossibly far and the ground grew steeper. Firewind began to slow.

'They're gaining on us,' he gasped. 'We'll never make it.'

Just as he spoke, the Etins seemed to hesitate. One by one they came to a halt and the hail of stones ceased. Peter stared over his shoulder in wonder. Then he saw first one then another slowly topple over. Though it was difficult through the morning haze, he fancied he could just make out a faint brightness hovering over each of the fallen grey forms.

'It's all right,' he gasped. 'Loriana must have let some of the Naida remain behind. We're safe!'

To Peter's relief they made the ridge and crossed out of sight down into the other side. Only then did Firewind slow his pace.

Still bathed in the dawn shadow of the mountain, the vast dark swathe of the Great Forest stretched before them.

'At least we'll be safe there – for the moment,' said Peter with a sigh of relief. 'Come on, Firewind. Let's go down.'

* * *

Sarah awoke that same morning feeling very unsettled in herself. She had worried all night about those animals who had not come into the Enchanted Glade. Surely not all of them could be evil, she thought to herself. They must just be fooled by those hares and by the wizards.

She rose from her mossy bed and, careful to wake nobody else, made for the entrance to the Enchanted Glade.

When she reached the sentinel stones that marked the gap, she hesitated. If she left the safety of the glade, would she be able to get back? Cautiously, she put one foot over the threshold. She had no difficulty in returning it. Plucking up courage, she stepped outside. To her relief, she found she could re-enter just as easily.

Satisfied that she could return in safety, Sarah set off to find as many animals as she could. She would try to persuade them to enter the glade for themselves.

What struck her almost immediately was the unnatural silence. Normally she would have expected at least some of the forest-folk to be bustling about their early morning business. However, there was nobody in sight.

Puzzled by this, she walked further on. All the while, she kept her eyes open not only for friendly animals but also for hares. She realised that she was taking a big risk in coming out like this and after a short while began to wish she had spoken to Trotter first. The silence was eerie and she wondered what had become of all the animals. Perhaps Terras and Sorda had put a spell on them and turned them to stone. Maybe the mysterious hunter had killed them all.

The further she went, the more Sarah was filled with trepidation. Her early desire to save some of the animals evaporated like water off a hot stone. She decided to return to the glade.

However, she had retraced only a dozen or so steps when she saw a flicker of movement ahead. She stopped and stared. Her body tensed ready to flee.

'Who are you?' she called anxiously. 'Show yourself.'

There was no reply.

Then suddenly, a man stepped silently from behind a tree not twenty metres from where Sarah stood. He wore garments of mottled shades of brown and green. In his hands he held a bow and arrow.

Without a word, he drew back the string.

The arrow pointed straight at Sarah's heart.

13

Sad Partings

Sarah looked death in the face for the second morning in a row.

She felt strangely unafraid, almost calm. There was no uncertainty, no lurking fear of the unexpected. She only hoped that the arrow would find its mark and that she would die instantly and without much pain. Yet she might still play for time.

'Who are you?' she called. 'Why do you want to kill me?'

'I am called Duron,' replied the bowman. 'I am in the employ of Feldrog the Almighty, the Lord of the Universe.' He paused. 'Your name is Sarah, is it not?'

She nodded.

'You are a fool to have stayed in the forest. Why did you not leave when you had the opportunity to do so?'

'That's my business,' Sarah replied. 'I don't know who this Feldrog is but he sounds to me like no friend of Oswain's – and he's the real ruler of the Great Forest. You have no right. . . .' Suddenly, it dawned on Sarah who the stranger was. 'You . . . you're the one who has been killing all the animals. You're the terrorist!' she cried. 'How can anyone be so . . . so evil?'

Sarah's fists clenched in rage and, forgetting her own

danger, she glowered at her adversary.

Duron laughed coldly.

'Oswain is dead, and so are his soft-headed ways. The future belongs to Feldrog. Before long, every kingdom and every knee in the world will bow in his honour,' he declared. 'Tomorrow the Great Forest will fall, and no one can prevent it – least of all you, or the old fools you support. And as for the so-called Guild of the White Eagle – what a joke!'

'I don't believe you!' cried Sarah, though her tone of voice betrayed her doubts.

'Whether you do or not will hardly matter because, unfortunately, you won't be here to find out,' he sneered. 'You have served your purpose. Prepare to die, young wench! This time you really won't escape!'

Sarah fixed her eyes on the unwavering arrow. Would she have time to dodge it? She had no idea how fast a real arrow travelled. Which way should she dive? Would he have another arrow ready before she could find cover?

Duron's fingers flexed as he prepared to loose the fatal shaft.

Just when Sarah thought the last moment of her life had arrived, a sudden thudding sound filled the air. Duron heard it too and he hesitated. Suddenly, he span round. A powerful chestnut stallion was thundering through the trees straight towards him. Clinging to his neck for dear life was a boy Sarah recognised at once as her brother.

It all happened so quickly. Before Duron could do

anything to save himself the horse struck him full on the chest and he was crushed beneath the pitiless hooves that thundered over him. His proud bow was broken and his arrows scattered uselessly across the ground.

Peter slithered from his mount and, with scarcely a backward glance at the fallen killer, he ran towards his sister.

'Peter! Oh, Peter!' she cried, as she flung herself gratefully into his arms. He held her for a long time while she sobbed out all the pain and fear she had felt.

At last she calmed and could look him in the face. She smiled and sniffed. 'You came just in time,' she said. 'I didn't even know you were here.'

Peter's face was grim and tense, but he smiled back and affectionately wiped a tear from his sister's cheek. 'Sorry I haven't got a handkerchief, sis,' he replied. 'You look like you need one.'

She gave a rueful laugh.

'I've only just come,' Peter explained. 'Firewind brought me. He's Oswain's horse.'

'Then Oswain is all right?' Sarah asked hopefully.

Peter nodded. 'Injured, but OK. Loriana's gone to help him. I was sent here; then I've got to go to Elmar.'

They turned to where Duron lay dead. Firewind grazed quietly nearby. Peter called him and introduced him to Sarah. Then Peter went across to Duron. Gold coins were scattered on the ground. He picked one up and it glinted coldly in the morning light. For a moment he was tempted to collect them all up. Then it struck him how worthless it all was compared to life itself.

Blood money. With a sigh, he rose and returned empty-handed to Sarah and Firewind.

'We need to talk,' he said tersely.

It took about an hour for the three of them to exchange all their news.

'We'd better find out what's happened to all the other animals,' said Peter. 'Then we must get back to Trotter and tell him the news.'

'I don't think he's going to be too pleased with me, though,' Sarah said ruefully. 'I should have told him where I was going.'

'He'd have been less pleased if you'd got yourself killed,' Peter retorted. 'Come on, let's go.'

It took them very little time to come across the stockade. Sitting together astride Firewind, and hidden by the trees, they stared in amazement at the sight. They could see hares on the battlements standing guard with their spears and even caught a glimpse of Terras and Sorda. The gates were open but heavily guarded. Although they could see many animals inside the stockade, none ventured out.

Without a word they withdrew and set off in the direction of the Enchanted Glade.

Their arrival caused a tremendous commotion among the forest-folk.

Sarah's disappearance had, naturally, perturbed Trotter, but he was relieved to see her return. She apologised to him for going off without telling him. He looked grave when she told him of Duron and the way he had fallen beneath Firewind's hooves.

Everyone wanted to hear Peter's news and they cheered aloud when he told them that Oswain was alive and now in the safe hands of the Barkums. They became even more excited when Firewind reported their meeting with the Ice Maiden. Fumble did a perfect backward somersault to express his delight.

However, when Peter explained about Feldrog and just how close he was to the Great Forest, everyone grew very solemn indeed.

'What are we going to do, Trotter?' Grumble asked the old badger. It was the question everyone wished to be answered.

Trotter rose and walked slowly backwards and forwards stroking his grey whiskers.

'That I do not easily know,' he replied thoughtfully. 'Peter, of course, must continue on to Elmar without delay. That is Oswain's wish.' He sighed heavily. 'As for ourselves, I am less sure. It now seems obvious to me that this Duron and those wretched wizards were in the plot together. That means the wizards are working for Feldrog and all this nonsense about a republic is just a ruse.'

'It looks to me as though all the animals with them are prisoners without realising it,' said William the hedgehog.

'Precisely,' piped up Mumble. 'All Feldrog has to do is march straight to the stockade and there they are waiting to be captured, or worse.'

'Then our duty is plain,' said Trotter decisively. 'We must warn the animals and give them the opportunity to escape and join us. Does everyone agree?'

The company nodded their assent.

'But will we be safe here, even in the Enchanted Glade?' asked Flip-flop the rabbit.

'Even if we are, it's going to be like being in prison ourselves,' offered another. 'We might be protected from Feldrog but we won't be able to do anything to help anyone else.'

Trotter was clearly unsure what to do.

'I want to discuss this with Peter and Sarah,' he said. 'We'll meet again in about half an hour.'

When he had dismissed the company he addressed the two children.

'They're right, you know. We will be like an island in the middle of an angry sea, and who knows if the waves won't overwhelm us? Yet I am loath to leave this place. It is our home, you see.'

Peter and Sarah nodded.

'I suppose Oswain and Loriana won't get here in time?' Peter wondered.

Trotter shrugged. 'Who can say? Maybe Loriana can heal him at once, maybe not. Yet, even if he arrives, what then? The forest-folk are divided. If Loriana is right, then Feldrog will be here by nightfall. How can we hope to rally what little forces we have in such a short time, even with Oswain to lead us?'

'I would like to look into Elmere,' said Sarah. 'Maybe that will tell us something.'

Trotter brightened at the suggestion, and agreed.

It did not take them long to discover the awful truth.

As the three of them gazed into the pool they saw three bright golden stars. Abruptly, one of them disappeared. At once, the surface of the pool rippled and the scene changed. They saw trees falling – not just one or two, but hundreds upon hundreds. The message was unmistakable.

Sarah felt sick at the sight and turned away.

'There is only one thing for it,' said Trotter. He was suddenly decisive. 'Once we have given the animals in the stockade a chance to escape, we must flee the forest and make for Elmar. We may not make it, but if we do we may yet be of some use. There is nothing to be gained by remaining here.'

Peter agreed, and said that he would get horses and carts to come out from Elmar to meet the animals and speed them on their journey.

At this, Sarah turned violently. Her face was aghast.

'Peter, what are you saying? Have you forgotten? What about Andrew? We can't just run away and leave him to Feldrog. He's our brother!'

Peter didn't know what to say. He lowered his eyes before Sarah's accusing gaze.

Trotter intervened gently. 'Sarah, I know it is difficult, perhaps more difficult than anything else in the world, but you cannot save Andrew by yourselves. Even with all our help it would be hopeless. We are outnumbered thousands to one.' He put a comforting paw on her arm.

'That doesn't mean we shouldn't try!' she cried hotly. 'We've always stuck together. I'd sooner die than be a coward!'

'Sarah . . .' Peter began.

'It's all right for you, Peter. You've got your orders,' she snapped. 'You too, Trotter. You're responsible for all these forest-folk. But what am I to do? I can't just run away. I just can't.'

With that she burst into tears and stumbled away, leaving Trotter and Peter standing helpless beside the pool.

* * *

'She's right, of course,' said Trotter after Sarah had left. 'But it would be suicide to remain.' He shook his head. 'It is a hard choice.'

However, there was nothing they could do for Sarah at present since preparations had to be made for the approach to the stockade.

It was agreed that the forest-folk would go in strength, fully armed and ready if necessary to fight. They would announce the news of Oswain's expected return and offer help to all who wished to rejoin them. After that, the forest-folk would begin their journey to Elmar.

It was mid-afternoon. The sun shone warmly on the fresh grass. Flowers bloomed in abundance and honey bees buzzed lazily from one blossom to another, while butterflies flitted in the light breeze. Nobody would have thought anything was amiss in the Great Forest.

Yet it was a grim-faced company that set out from the Enchanted Glade. Trotter led the way, closely followed by Peter and Sarah and his trusty retainers. A great crowd followed. They were ready for a fight.

It was obvious that Terras and Sorda were expecting them, for the gates of the stockade were closed fast and hares armed with spears lined the barricade.

Andrew read the sign on the gate. 'More like hell on earth,' he observed.

Trotter nodded. 'When will folk learn that heaven is a gift to be received from Elmesh and not something they can build for themselves?' he said.

'So have you come to give yourselves up?' sneered Terras from above the ramparts.

'Throw down your weapons if that is the case,' demanded Sorda.

'We have come to do nothing of the sort,' replied Trotter with dignity. 'Instead we offer the forest-folk a last chance.' His aged voice grew with unexpected strength. 'Now hear this, all you forest-folk who dwell under the reign of Oswain. The King lives! Soon he will return. A pardon is offered to all who will turn from their treachery and follow him.'

At this the hares jeered in unison and one or two spears were thrown in Trotter's direction.

'I have more to say,' declared Trotter, undaunted by their response. 'This very day the forest will be invaded by a cruel tyrant. You have been fooled by your advisers into entering this . . . this prison. The republic is a lie. It has lured you into a trap. He will capture every one of you if you remain. Escape while you can. In the name of Elmesh I beg you not to stay here. You can come with us.'

'What is this nonsense?' jeered Terras in reply. 'With one breath the old fool claims that Oswain is returning alive; with another he tells us that a tyrant will invade the forest. Believe that and you'll believe anything!'

'You speak like an old fool,' cried the hare, whom Sarah recognised as the chief judge. 'This is nothing but a ruse to get us to open our gates and fall to your treachery. We will not heed you.'

The badger appealed to them again but got only the same response.

There was nothing more to be said. Trotter and his followers withdrew a short distance and waited to see what would happen.

For a while all was still. Then they heard a commotion coming from inside the stockade.

Peter started. 'Perhaps there's a revolution,' he said. 'Maybe they're fighting the wizards.'

Everyone waited in anticipation. Suddenly, figures appeared on the top of the stockade. Some kind of struggle was taking place.

Then, to everyone's horror, a young badger was cast to the ground. A fox and a rabbit followed. Several others were thrown down. They lay wounded and bleeding at the foot of the stockade.

Then Sorda appeared.

'Here are your loyal followers,' he sneered. 'Traitors, every one of them. You can have them back!'

Trotter's company stared aghast at the sight.

'We must help them,' said Trotter at once. 'It will be risky, because they will strike us with spears if they can. But we must help.'

'I'll take that risk,' said Peter. He looked steadily at the fallen animals. 'I'm not afraid.'

'Ride on my back, Peter. We'll go in fast,' said Firewind.

Trotter nodded. 'We'll give you covering fire,' he said.

So it was that Peter and Firewind, heedless of their own safety, ran the gauntlet of spears. One by one they rescued the helpless forest-folk who lay at the foot of the stockade. Trotter's company threw spears and fired arrows each time the pair raced to rescue another stricken animal. Altogether they saved nine lives.

* * *

They had not long returned to the safety of the Enchanted Glade when they heard the first explosion. Everyone looked up. A cloud of white smoke arose from the eastern skyline. In the silence that followed, the distant crackle of falling trees could be faintly but clearly heard.

'Etins,' said Peter grimly. 'They've reached the forest.'

'It is time we were leaving,' said Trotter quietly. 'Fumble, gather the folk. We move out in ten minutes.'

Leaving the Enchanted Glade was one of the saddest moments imaginable. Trotter led the way. Because of his frailty and the need for speed, he had reluctantly consented to being pushed in a wooden wheelchair by two weasels and a fox. There were tears in his old eyes as he took one last look at the Star Pool.

The Merestone remained. That could not be removed. However, Trotter carried with him the Book of Truth. It was all he took of his worldly possessions, for there was nothing else of real importance to him. In one final moment of private sorrow he stood beside the grave of his departed wife, Mrs Trotter. Then, silently, he left.

Hundreds of animals followed, old and young alike, most carrying few belongings. Speed was what mattered now. No one smiled. More explosions echoed across the trees and the noise of falling timber became frequent.

Once everyone was safely on the way, Trotter called Peter to his side.

'You must ride on now,' he said. 'Send transport if you can, but stop for nothing. It is vital that you reach Elmar as soon as possible. Do not worry if we fail to make it. At least we will die fighting.' He grasped Peter's hand. 'Elmesh be with you, my friend. Good speed.'

Peter nodded solemnly and, fighting back the tears, mounted Firewind.

At once, eager to obey Oswain's command, the horse was off. Too late Peter realised that he had not said goodbye to his sister. He had last seen her shepherding some of the younger voles into line. She would understand. Now he had to concentrate on the journey ahead.

He must ride like the wind.

But Sarah was no longer with the party of refugees. Once she was sure everyone was together, she had quietly slipped away. Now, back in the Enchanted Glade, she stood alone beside the Merestone. Her mind was made up. She would rescue Andrew or die in the attempt.

Half an hour later, the ground trembled beneath her feet. Startled, she looked around to see what was causing it. Then she heard the sound of running water. With a gasp, she watched as the Star Pool slowly drained away. Soon there remained only an empty stone basin. It was split right through the middle.

Sarah felt afraid.

By now it was growing towards evening and the light was fading. One by one, the early stars peeked through the azure sky as the sun sank in an orange haze to the West. That was where Elmar lay, where there was safety and friendship – for the moment, at least.

She gazed at the Merestone. The shadow had grown and its light seemed subdued. Now it flickered, then appeared to glow more brightly. Somehow its colouring looked different. Sarah watched, mesmerised.

Then she heard a loud crack which made her jump. Before her astonished gaze, the Merestone suddenly freed itself from the rock and began to hover in the air. Just as suddenly, it started to drift upwards, slowly at first, but with gathering speed. Then, with a faint whoosh, it accelerated into the fading sky like a meteorite going in the wrong direction.

Sarah stared after it, and her heart ached unbearably. She felt she knew its destination. The Merestone was returning to the place of its birth, to Elrilion, the star of Elmesh.

In the gathering gloom she walked away. There was nothing to remain for. The days of the Enchanted Glade were over. All alone in the world, Sarah, with solemn resolve, went out to meet her destiny.

Even as she passed between them, the great sentinel stones toppled to the ground and the wind blew chill across a dying world.

14

The Road to Elmar

The road to Elmar was three days' journey, but Peter intended to do it in two. Firewind seemed tireless and galloped furiously through the forest once they had left Trotter.

By nightfall, they had picked up the main highway and were crossing the bleak Waste Plains to the west of the Great Forest. Peter realised that Feldrog would probably make use of the same road too. It was not a pleasant thought and he wondered just how long it would take before his vast armies surrounded the capital city of the West.

High on the empty moorland road, Firewind ate up the miles and Peter wondered at the power of his steed. Any normal horse would have tired by now. Yet the stock of Arandell was special: these were the great stallions and mares created by Elmesh from the beginning. Most, by mingling with lesser breeds, had lost such strength, but a few could trace their descent by unbroken bloodline from the beginning. Firewind was one such.

At first the sky was clear and stars sparkled like a million living diamonds so that the road shone cold but distinct through the darkness. However, as time passed, gathering cloud began to dim the stars and the air grew sultry.

The storm broke with a violent flash of jagged lightning that lit up the northern horizon. A reverberating crash of thunder rolled across the moors. Another flash floodlit the sky, and another. It made Peter feel very exposed on the high open road.

Then the first heavy drops of rain began to fall. Within minutes, it was impossible to see a thing through the torrential downpour. Reluctantly, Firewind slowed his pace to a trot.

'I fear you will be thrown if we carry on and I lose the path,' he panted.

Peter agreed. Shivering in the heavy rain, he clung to Firewind's neck for warmth as slowly they pushed on through the downpour. Peter wondered how Trotter and his company were faring in this storm. If Elmesh was on their side it seemed a strange way of showing it!

'Of all the stupid times to have a storm!' he muttered.

The rain seemed to go on for ever and Peter had no idea how far he and Firewind had travelled. When it did finally abate he was surprised to see that they had almost reached the boundary of the Waste Plains. The mountain range that separated the realm of Elmar from that of the Great Forest loomed near.

'This is better,' said Firewind. 'Now we must make up for lost time.'

With that he broke into a gallop once more and before long they were climbing the winding road into the mountains. At one time this pass had been treacherous, but now the road was well used and even at its highest point there was little to fear. On only one occasion did Firewind have to slow down because the rain had turned to ice underfoot.

Peter felt absolutely exhausted. By early dawn, they were descending the far side of the mountain and, in spite of his efforts not to, he fell asleep on Firewind's back.

The unexpected sound of a dog barking jerked him from his slumber.

He sat upright with a jolt. Firewind had come to a halt. To his dismay, Peter saw at once that they were surrounded by rank upon rank of heavily armed cavalry. The worst had happened. With a groan of defeat, he slumped forward again onto Firewind's neck. He could hear the soldiers laughing.

'Well, that's a fine way to greet an old mate, I must say!' barked a voice from the ground.

'Yes, old bean. Manners and all that, what?' said another.

Without lifting his head Peter opened his eyes and stared. He recognised the dogs at once.

'Tatters! How did you get here?' he cried. 'And Hercules! Then . . .'

'That's right,' said a strong man's voice. 'You are with the armies of Kraan, Peter. Welcome!'

Peter sat up again and found himself looking into the steady eyes of Surin of Traun, the king of the realm of Kraan. They were old allies.*

---

*You can read all about this in *Oswain and the Quest for the Ice Maiden*.

'Why . . . th-this is amazing,' he stammered. 'I thought for a moment that you were Boribars, or . . . or Feldrog's men.' He wiped a hand across his face. 'I feared the worst.'

Surin smiled grimly. 'Dangers abound, but nothing is altogether lost while we still have breath within us,' he replied. 'Well met, Peter.' He nudged alongside and extended his hand. Peter took it, still stunned.

'What are you doing here?' he asked. 'I was supposed to ride to Elmar and get them to send messengers to you. They had to tell you what was happening and ask you to bring your army to Elmar as quickly as possible.'

'Are you the only folk who hear the voice of Elmesh?' Surin asked searchingly. His dark eyes were penetrating and Peter recognised that though he was a totally changed ruler from what he had once been, he remained a stern figure of great power.

'N-no,' he answered. 'I just thought . . .'

'We have known of Feldrog's plans for some time. Messages reached us and then refugees began to pour into Traun for safety. Oswain, we knew, was missing, but we have been in constant touch with Princess Alena and with the King and Queen in Elmar. What we did not know was whether Feldrog would turn north to attack us or whether we should come to the aid of the Great Forest, or even Elmar itself.'

'So what did you decide?'

'It was not easy. Our wise met and consulted Elmesh as best we knew. Then one had a dream. You know him well, and he is here.'

Peter looked up.

'Karador! You as well!' he exclaimed. 'This is wonderful.'

'Greetings, Peter,' said a tall dark-skinned man on a grey mare. He extended his hand. 'In my vision I saw only an open road. The sun rose at one end of the road. It passed quickly over to set at the other end. I knew then that it must run from east to west. Then I saw a horse racing along the road. That was all.'

Surin took up the story again. 'When I heard this from Lord Karador I knew that we should trust the safety of our realm and bring our armies down to this road. On our arrival we planned to turn either towards the Great Forest or towards Elmar.' He glanced at Karador apologetically. 'You saw well, my friend. I never expected to see the horse – even less Oswain's steed, and ridden by Peter. Truly the events of these days are far beyond our powers.'

'It's just amazing,' said Peter. 'You couldn't have come at a better time. We need your help so much.'

He and Firewind quickly explained as much as they could of the events to date. Surin's face was grim when he was told of the tragedy of the Great Forest, though he cheered to hear of Oswain's safety.

'It will grieve him greatly to lose his kingdom,' he said. 'Nevertheless, our duty is clear. Elmesh has spoken. We will send help to Trotter and his company. Chariots will be speediest. The main army will march to Elmar with all haste. You, Peter, must ride on to prepare the way.' He laughed. 'Alas, we have no horse to match your speed, Firewind.'

Surin gave immediate orders to his troops. Karador would lead the party to assist Trotter. He was to take with him a strong guard. Tatters and Hercules, together with the other hounds, would run with him. They were to deal ruthlessly with Boribar attacks. Meanwhile, the fastest troops were to go ahead with Surin to Elmar so that a council of war could take place upon their arrival. The rest would be no more than half a day behind. Peter hoped to reach the capital by late afternoon that day.

Greatly cheered by this unexpected meeting, Peter and Firewind bade farewell to their allies and with renewed energies raced on towards the city of Elmar.

* * *

Sarah left the Enchanted Glade behind with a sense of sadness too deep for words. Yet somehow she knew that the departure of the Merestone was something that had to take place. Time was marching on and events greater than she could understand or control were coming to pass. All that mattered to her now was to do what she thought was right; to be true to herself and true to her brother. That, she believed, was the will of Elmesh.

In that frame of mind, she made her way eastwards, carefully skirting Aldred's Park as she did so. She would dearly have liked to pay her last respects at the statue of the stoat who long ago had given his life to save hers, but she knew that it was too close to the stockade. She could not risk being captured by Terras and Sorda. But she thought about him as she walked. Maybe she had to do something similar to save Andrew. It seemed very different to choose to give your life for someone you loved, rather than to have it snatched away by injustice or terrorism, she thought.

The noise of the Etins' work continued into the night and Sarah had little difficulty in following the sound through the otherwise silent forest.

Several hours passed, and the wind began to rise. Trees swayed and rustled. It was no longer quite so easy to find her direction. Then there was a sudden flash of lightning followed by a far-off rumble of thunder. Before long, an electrical storm was raging overhead. Sarah hoped that the trees wouldn't be struck.

It started to rain. At first she was fairly sheltered but before long torrents started to pour through the branches overhead and she soon became soaked to the skin. It was difficult to see where she was going, and the roar of the rain made it impossible to hear the Etins.

As the wild wind and the pouring rain continued, branches began to fall from the trees. Sarah realised that with the departure of the Merestone the forest was no longer a safe place to be. Shivering with cold she took shelter beneath a solid-looking oak and hoped that she would be all right until the storm passed.

She must have fallen asleep, for when she came to herself, dawn had broken. Cold, wet and stiff, she struggled to her feet, relieved to find that the storm was over and only a few light, fluffy clouds broke the fresh sky.

From the sound of it, the Etins were already at work building the fateful road into the Great Forest. Struggling to her feet, Sarah started on the last stage of her journey.

When she finally came upon them, she could hardly believe her eyes. Peter had given her some description of the giants but she had not realised just how monstrous they were. She watched in awe as the huge creatures lumbered along carrying great lumps of rock as though they were made of papier mâché. Some used massive boulders to hammer the road flat and she marvelled at their strength. Certainly she wanted to keep out of their way!

Skirting round this scene of noisy activity, she spied through the trees the way the road snaked up into the mountains. But what really caught her eye was the sight at the top of the pass. At this distance, all she could see was a glowing pink shell and gold glittering in the morning light, but she knew at once what it was.

'Feldrog!' she breathed to herself. 'Peter was right. He's here already.'

She wondered whether to go further on but then thought better of it. Feldrog would reach here before long, anyway. She would save her strength until she needed it.

So Sarah sat and watched as the procession slowly descended the mountain and entered the forest.

She wondered why there were no children pulling the chariot as Peter had suggested. Then she realised that they were at the rear, holding it back against the slope. Behind them followed what looked to be an endless army. She could hear music playing. Feldrog made no secret of his coming, that was for sure.

It wasn't long before she lost sight of the great chariot-throne among the trees as it reached the foot of the mountain. Sarah roused herself and started towards it, though still keeping to the cover of the trees as she walked parallel to the road.

Once she came in sight of the cavalcade again, she could see the hundreds of children who now toiled on the ropes. Stern-looking overseers wielded whips to ensure that nobody slacked. Somewhere in that number was her brother, but try as she might she couldn't spot him.

Sarah had given very little thought to her own safety beyond keeping out of sight, but as the chariot drew near she became aware of the awesome power of Feldrog. From her hidden vantage point she gazed on the tyrant-king. He was not what she had expected. His dark face was handsome and he looked strong and alert. He sat erect on his exalted throne and his cool gaze surveyed everything before him. There was no mistaking the aura of irresistible power that surrounded him. Sarah felt the unwanted tinge of fear even as she looked. She determined that she would not lose her nerve. Instead, she concentrated on searching for Andrew among the children.

Her chance to act came unexpectedly. At a nod from Feldrog, the cavalcade came to a standstill. He arose from his throne and descended the stairs, before disappearing somewhere to the rear. The overseers, judging that none of the children would run away, joined him. Sarah wondered if they had stopped to eat, though she saw no sign of food for the children.

She decided to seize the opportunity. Running as fast as she could she could she scrambled up onto the road and mingled among the children. Most of them seemed somewhat bemused at her sudden presence but no one made a move to stop her.

'Andrew? Andrew? Where are you?' she hissed.

Then she spotted him. His clothes were ragged and dirty, but there was no mistaking his face. Weaving through the ranks of children, and clambering over the white tow ropes, she hastened towards him.

'Andrew!' she cried breathlessly. 'I've found you!' She flung her arms around him. He stared at her in stunned disbelief.

'Sarah! How did you get here? I didn't think you had even arrived in this world,' he gasped.

'There's no time to explain now,' she answered. 'Come on, we've got to get away from here.'

She tugged urgently at his sleeve.

He lowered his eyes and removed her hand.

'I can't, Sarah. Really I can't. Sorry. Go on – you escape while you can,' he replied dully.

'What do you mean?' she said. Her eyes opened wide with incredulity. She looked for ropes, or chains and fetters, but saw none.

'I'm sorry,' he repeated. 'I'm just too scared. It-it's

Feldrog . . . I can't explain.'

Try as she might, and she tried desperately, Sarah just couldn't persuade her brother to leave.

Suddenly, she was aware that the other children around were taking an interest. One in particular elbowed his way forward. He was a large, fat boy.

'Who's she?' he demanded belligerently. 'What's she up to?'

'Oh it's you, Gumboil,' said Andrew. 'This is my sister, Sarah. She wants me to escape.'

'What? Don't be stupid. You'll never get away,' he said scornfully. 'Anyway, we'll all be in trouble if you go.'

Then, to Sarah's horror, he started shouting. 'Hey, there's someone here trying to rescue a prisoner. Hey!'

Other children took up the cry, and Sarah despaired of rescuing her brother.

The commotion ceased as suddenly as it had started. All at once the children became totally silent. Their ranks drew back, leaving Sarah standing all alone. Feldrog gazed down at her from the height of his chariot. In his hand he held a slender gold rod sharpened at the point like a needle. With a knowing smile curling around his lips, he beckoned Sarah.

15

Betrayed by Wizards

Instantly, Sarah felt as if she had been stung by a wasp. She cried out in agony, but the pain continued. Gasping, she writhed on the ground, begging for the torment to end.

Just as suddenly, the pain ceased. Then Sarah knew that she was afraid, deeply and terribly frightened.

Feldrog spoke no words, but she heard his voice.

'Fool you are, to think that I did not know,' he said. 'Hark, your friends are fleeing to Elmar. The rest of the dwellers in this realm are shut up in Aldred's Park. You came to rescue your brother. I have watched you, Sarah Brown. I have known you all along. Even the death of Duron is known to me.'

Sarah quailed. Was there any secret hidden from this man? She thought not, but lest there was any doubt, he continued: 'Oswain – too. He is not here to greet me. That is unfortunate, but he will bow nonetheless just as soon as I reach Elmar, where doubtless I will find him! Your other brother rides to warn of my coming.' He flashed a smile. 'It is amusing.'

An overseer spoke.

'Mighty Lord of All, King of the Ages, Eternal Master, shall I have her join the ranks of these unworthy scum

175

privileged to convey your majesty to his destiny, or do you wish her flogged to death?'

Feldrog gazed on the girl sprawled helplessly before him.

'I think not.' He spoke aloud now, smoothly, with absolute authority. 'She is pleasing to behold. She shall join the dancing girls and see my triumph with her own eyes. Clothe her suitably. Since she is a companion of those who soon shall bow to me, she shall stand by my right hand to observe their humiliation.'

Trembling with fear, Sarah stumbled to her feet. She had lost sight of Andrew. Her hopes were dashed and her fate seemed sealed.

Yet a small spark still smouldered. She had, of her own will, obeyed her conscience. Deep down inside, she was free. In spite of her terrible dread, Sarah determined not to lose that spark.

* * *

The Etins made terrifyingly easy progress through the Great Forest. Their huge arms tore trees from the ground as if they were no more than tufts of grass. It wasn't long before they had smashed out a broad swathe all the way to Aldred's Park. Boulders carried from the mountains were slammed into the rain-softened earth and beaten level under the giants' feet. Feldrog's road had cut to the very heart of Oswain's kingdom.

Panic broke out within the stockade at the first sight of the giants. Even the arrogant hares began to realise their folly as they gazed in awe at the approaching monsters. Only Terras and Sorda remained unmoved. Indeed, both appeared to be very contented with the way matters were progressing.

Fear led to fighting as the crowded animals sought to escape from the compound. Some – rabbits, moles, rats and the like – began burrowing into the ground as fast as they could, but they kept getting pushed over by the heaving tide of animals who rushed blindly this way and that.

Those who tried to scramble up the walls were either pulled down by others who wanted the space or were repelled by the dutiful hares who guarded the battlements. Many were trampled underfoot but their cries for help were lost in the shouting and yelling. In the end, out of the confusion, a group organised by a fox named Raban marched up to where the wizards stood observing the scene from above the gate.

'What's going on?' demanded the fox. 'You promised us we would be safe here and we believed you. Huh! Safe from a girl, maybe, but certainly not from those giants! Why, it would take only a matter of moments for them to crush us all to pulp. We can't stay here. It's like a prison. Let us go free so that we can take our chance in the open forest. Open the gates while we've still time!'

Terras sneered at the deputation.

'How quickly you change your tune,' he said in a voice heavy with sarcasm. 'We save you from that evil girl who sought to pick you off one by one. We offer you protection. We freely make available our wisdom and guidance. And what do you do? You throw it back in our faces at the first hint of what you think is danger. Fools! Do you really think those great creatures are interested in you? No, they chase a much greater prize than you could ever imagine.'

'I don't believe you,' piped up a female mole. 'Maybe that old badger was right after all. We're trapped here and it's our own silly fault. We had a chance and we threw it away. Now it's too late.' She began to wail uncontrollably.

Some of those who stood nearby tried to silence her, but others joined the wailing. Soon confusion reigned on every side and the meeting ended in uproar.

'Silence!' cried Terras, but nobody listened.

Animals were rushing around everywhere. Even the hares now wanted to escape. It was obvious that at any moment they would charge the gate and scramble up the walls in such numbers that it would be impossible to stop them.

Sorda reached into his robe and drew out a slender black wand. Slowly, he traced a circle in the air. Then he pointed it at the churning mass of animals below. He traced another circle.

The effect was stunning. Those animals climbing the walls suddenly fell to the ground. The ones trying to dig their way out felt their strength fail and they flopped helplessly on their faces. Everyone quietened.

Then Sorda spoke.

'Foolish, isn't it?' he sneered. 'You fear the giants, but they are only minor servants. One far greater comes behind them. He is to be your king. Him you will honour.' Sorda drew himself upright. 'There is no one to match the Master of the Universe. He is Feldrog, the Eternal Glory.'

At this the animals were silent as the impact of his words sunk in.

He continued, 'How else shall such a one be welcomed, except by all his subjects? That is why you are honoured to be here in one place. Your eyes will be privileged to see the Great Ruler in his splendour. You will beg to pay him homage, for there is none like him.'

Then, as Sorda finished speaking, the sound of a single trumpet blast echoed through the trees. A loud fanfare followed. Without a word, the animals in the stockade bowed themselves to the ground.

* * *

Standing high on Feldrog's chariot, Sarah stared glumly in front of her. She was clothed like all the other dancing girls in a long flowing skirt and a short top, but she did not feel like dancing. Feldrog had stood her just one step down from the dais where he sat so that she should see best his conquest of Oswain's kingdom. Silent and helpless, she watched with deep sadness the destruction of the forest and the steady advance of the road.

Feldrog watched too. He sat back easily on his throne. His face was smug and a satisfied smile curled around his lips. One of the dancing girls fed him peeled grapes while another anointed his feet with oil. He sipped from a flagon of wine. This was a simple victory.

Slowly the chariot rolled forward as the children bent their backs to the ropes. Sarah could see Andrew down there among all the others. She felt guilty about being in this hateful place of honour beside Feldrog while her brother toiled below, but there was nothing she could do about it. Feldrog's rule was absolute and the terrible fear that gripped her forbade any disagreement. She never wanted to feel his Sting again.

It was just before noon when they came in sight of the stockade. Sarah wondered at the madness that had caused the animals to forsake their loyalty to Elmesh and to Oswain. If only they had listened to Trotter. It was all clear to her now. Feldrog had hired Duron the Hunter to unsettle the forest-folk. His lightning attacks, the silent unexpected arrows, had made everyone frightened and suspicious of one another.

With Oswain away and Trotter being so frail, it was all too easy for Terras and Sorda to get the hares on their side. What had they promised, she wondered? Power? Wealth? Position? Who could say? Whatever it was, it was sufficient to turn the forest into a place run by self-appointed police. Rules and regulations had replaced loyalty and trust. Threats of punishment rather than love for their friends and neighbours had made the forest-folk do as they were told. The rest had been simple.

Once the animals had become used to keeping the rules without really thinking about them, it was an easy task to persuade them to build the compound and follow their new leaders.

Sarah felt sick at heart. Terras and Sorda were giving Feldrog a gift. Instead of having to subdue the forest-folk scattered throughout the vast area of the Great Forest, Feldrog had only to come to this one place, and here they were, prisoners awaiting his pleasure. Trotter was right; the so-called republic – and Terras had called it the republic of heaven! – was just a clever trap.

Even as she thought about these things, the chariot drew to a halt in front of the stockade. With groans of relief the children let their ropes go slack. The vast army halted as regimental commanders shouted orders from rank to rank. Trumpets were blown and a rich fanfare sounded. The gates of the stockade opened and Terras and Sorda emerged to meet Feldrog. He rose from his throne and Sarah just hoped the wizards would not recognise her, standing as she was so close to him.

'Hail, O mighty Lord of All Things, Eternal Master, Ruler of the World,' cried Terras, with his hands raised in greeting. He promptly prostrated himself on the ground.

'Unworthy servants we are, O Most High One. We bring this small offering, a kingdom indeed, but hardly worthy of your excellent majesty,' cried Sorda. He too bowed himself to the ground.

Feldrog gazed without expression at the stockade. Then he stretched forth his Sting. For a moment nothing happened. Then the sign on the gates crumbled to dust and slowly the stakes that made up the defences began to fall outwards. One by one they hit the ground with a dull thud. Within a few moments the compound was no more.

Surrounded by a circle of fallen timber, hundreds upon hundreds of animals cowered to the earth in total silence. A cloud of dust drifted away in the morning breeze, leaving them totally at the mercy of Feldrog.

'So this is the heart of Oswain's kingdom,' said Feldrog. 'I am told that he is a great king. His lands are vast. Yet what pathetic subjects he rules!' He gazed around the clearing. 'Nevertheless, it shall not be altogether despised. I shall find use for it all, no doubt, if only for amusement.' He fastened his eyes on the wizards. 'Is this all you offer?' he enquired.

'Oh no, your Most Worthy Excellence,' answered Sorda. 'There is within the Enchanted Glade a stone of immense beauty and power. To take it would be beyond our most puny powers . . . .'

'Not that we would dare to do so since it is rightfully yours, O Most High One,' Terras interjected quickly.

'Yet it is not a match for your power, O Lord,' Sorda continued. 'Indeed, even now it awaits your pleasure.'

'Good, good,' mused Feldrog. A slight smile played about his lips. 'Then come, my good servants, take your reward.'

Sarah felt a little leap of joy at this. She wondered what would happen to the wizards when Feldrog discovered that the Merestone was in fact gone.

Feldrog glanced in her direction. She felt a pang of

fear course through her body. At once, she wanted to blurt out that the Merestone was no longer in the Enchanted Glade. She resisted as hard as she could, but the fear grew ever stronger.

'Do you think that I am going to hand you over to them?' he asked with a smirk.

Somehow, by a deep effort of her will, Sarah managed to switch her fear to that threat instead, so that she didn't have to think about the Merestone. It worked, and she waited in genuine fear as the wizards came forward.

However, instead of looking towards her, they had their eyes on the great piles of glittering diamonds that bedecked the floor of Feldrog's chariot. Greedily, they grasped huge handfuls and stuffed them into the recesses of their robes.

After a few moments, a glance from Feldrog indicated 'Enough!' Cowering, they made their way to the rear of his throne to join his vast entourage.

'Dance for me, or maybe I shall let them have you after all,' Feldrog murmured in Sarah's direction. 'It might make up for the fact that the Merestone has disappeared.'

With a shock of dismay she realised that, in spite of her efforts, he had read every one of her thoughts.

Feldrog faced the cowering animals.

'I, Feldrog, Lord of All Things, do hereby take possession of the Great Forest of Alamore. Every knee shall bow to me for all time and eternity. You and your descendants shall be my subjects for ever,' he proclaimed. 'And now we shall celebrate my glorious arrival with feasting, music and dancing.'

Thus for the remainder of that day Feldrog rested in Aldred's Park. Thousands upon thousands of soldiers poured in. Kitchens were set up, wine flowed freely and the revelry began. A long queue of animals stretched before the throne as one by one they came and bowed in homage to their new ruler.

Sarah joined the other girls and danced for Feldrog, fearing at any moment that he might deliver her into the cruel hands of the wizards. Only deep in her heart did she still hope that Trotter and the others might take advantage of this delay and make good their escape. Yet it seemed a very faint hope indeed.

16

Friends Meet

Towards evening, Peter came in sight of the twinkling lights that marked the city of Elmar.

'We're almost there, Firewind,' he panted. 'Well done.'

'I wish only that it could have been sooner,' panted the horse. 'Yet my master will not be unpleased.'

Soon they were galloping along the final straight stretch of road that led up to the city gates. Somewhere ahead, Peter spotted a white horse coming towards them.

'Slow down, Firewind,' he urged. 'Let's see what news the rider bears.'

As the horse drew nearer, he spied that the rider was a girl with long golden hair. She wore a dark green tunic braided with gold, and she carried a sword.

When they were about twenty lengths apart she raised her palm in greeting and came to a standstill.

'Hail, Peter! Hail, Firewind!' she cried. Her face broke into a wreath of smiles. Peter recognised her at once.

'Alena! How did you know we were coming, or did you just come out by chance?' he gasped as he drew level with the Princess.

She smiled, reached across and kissed him on the cheek.

185

'My mother, the Queen, still lives. There is little she does not discern,' she said knowingly. 'I thought I would come out to meet you myself.' She cocked her head to one side and grinned.

'Well, it's . . . it's really great to see you. Thanks for coming,' Peter replied. He suddenly felt good inside. 'I must look a bit of a mess,' he said, glancing down at his dust-covered clothes. 'It's been a long ride.'

Princess Alena laughed.

'Knowing you, Firewind, it must have been a very fast ride too!' she said, addressing the horse.

'I had my Master's orders, ma'am,' Firewind answered. 'I would go like the wind of a storm for him.'

'I know,' she said, and she patted his neck affectionately.

'Oswain is all right,' said Peter. 'I found him, and by now Loriana is probably by his side. I'll have to tell you all about it.'

'Elmesh be praised!' she exclaimed. 'My mother felt matters were suddenly well with her son, so it doesn't altogether surprise me. But it's good to hear it from someone who has actually seen him alive.'

Peter drew in his breath. 'That's about the only good news,' he said glumly. 'The rest is bad. Really bad.'

'We have expected something,' she answered solemnly. 'Tell me what you know while we ride back. Then you must appear before the King and Queen and repeat your news to them.'

Together, in the gathering gloom, they turned and rode towards the city that was destined to hold the last hope of their world.

* * *

Far away, in the depths of the woods and surrounded by the Barkums, Oswain slept. Loriana sat beside him and occasionally stroked his brow. Her face was thoughtful.

Since her meeting with Peter she had travelled quickly across country with the assistance of the Naida. Soon she came upon the woods and there she found the Boribars. Judging from their conversation they were searching for Oswain.

'He has to be here somewhere, so find him!' Atag shouted. 'How far can man get with broken leg, by thunder?'

'Unless it by sorcery,' growled one of the number. 'I don't much like this place. We should leave while we can.'

'What? And lose such a prize as this?' Atag spat contemptuously. 'I tell you he wish he never been born when I get hold of him. I break every bone in his body!'

Loriana had heard enough. She gave swift instructions to some of the Naida. Silently, they flitted through the trees until they came upon the tethered horses. In moments the beasts were freed and, without a sound, they followed the Naida out of the woods and onto the open plain. Riderless, they wandered far to the South, never to be seen again by their owners.

Then the Ice Maiden stepped fearlessly into the path of the Boribars. A halo of silver light surrounded her. The men stopped dead in their tracks.

'So, you seek Oswain, do you?' she said. 'Perhaps you wish to pay homage to the King. Though somehow I doubt that!'

Atag's hand flashed to his sword hilt.

'Who are you?' he growled.

The Ice Maiden gazed upon him with steely eyes.

'Who indeed?' she replied. 'I am the one who has searched long and hard for the man I love. Many times my heart has ached and I have felt lost and confused. Yet you have cruelly held him prisoner all this time.' Her gaze took in the others. 'You showed no mercy to an injured man. Should you now expect mercy?'

The rest of the Boribars trembled at her words. Surely here was the white witch of the woods, no less!

'It's Urga the Terrible!' cried one of the men.

Atag, however, stood his ground. He gave a coarse laugh.

'Who are you to offer mercy to us?' he scorned. 'You are but one mere woman against a whole gang.'

He drew his sword and made to step forward.

The Ice Maiden raised her hand. 'I am Loriana, the Ice Maiden, and King Oswain's consort,' she said. Then she spoke a few words in a strange tongue. At once, the Naida appeared and swiftly ringed the Boribars. Atag's sword fell to the ground. Sleep seemed irresistible.

'No, you shall not sleep,' she commanded. 'Instead, your punishment shall fit your crime. As you have given, so shall you receive. Lostness shall come upon you. Confusion and wandering shall be your lot. Thus you have chosen by your actions.'

At her words, one by one the Boribars began to walk quietly away, all in different directions. Soon they were completely out of sight.'

'Bravo! A splendid performance!' cried a voice.

Loriana turned to see the woody shape of Oakum emerging from the shadows. She smiled politely.

'Greetings, my Lady. I will take you to Oswain, if you wish,' said Oakum. 'I know the root.'

'I am sure you mean route,' said the Ice Maiden with a dry smile.

'That's what I said!'

So the Ice Maiden followed her strange guide until he brought her at last to a clearing where Oswain lay waiting. Weeping with joy and relief as their forced separation ended, they embraced one another tightly for a long time. It was a very personal moment.

'Perhaps we should leave them alone?' Sycum suggested discreetly.

'It would be best,' agreed Oakum, and the Barkums quietly withdrew to leave the couple undisturbed.

Oswain's leg proved to be in a bad way. With the help of the Naida, he was put into a deep sleep. Then, using her healing skills, the Ice Maiden carefully set the bones and applied special potions that she carried with her.

Later, as she sat beside him, she pondered the future. His kingdom would have fallen by now. It was a severe blow and she ached for the fate of the forest-folk. It would do little good to attempt a rescue mission. She knew that Feldrog had his sights set on Elmar itself. He would not remain long in the Great Forest.

She stroked Oswain's brow. Soon his leg would be mended and he would wake. They must make their plans with all haste.

* * *

Guards stood smartly to attention and saluted as Princess Alena and Peter passed through the city gates. She smiled in acknowledgement.

'They are fine men,' she said to Peter. 'Most of the royal guards were with me when we faced Surin on the battlefield.' She laughed. 'Things have changed so much since those days. I quite often go to visit him, and when affairs of state allow, he comes down here. Our two kingdoms trade together and everyone is pleased with the outcome.'

'I don't think the same is likely with Feldrog,' said Peter. 'He looks worse than your father ever was.'

They started up the main mall and Peter admired the fine buildings and leafy avenues of Elmar as they rode towards the palace. Lights sparkled from a myriad windows, and lamps burned at regular intervals along the way. Many people strolled together under the early evening stars and children played on the streets. Elmar was a city of peace and safety. He wondered how long it could remain so.

The palace lay straight ahead with its white turrets and towers, its balconies and bridges, ablaze with light.

As soon as they were through the palace gates, liveried footmen took charge of the horses. Peter and Alena ran up the marble steps that led to the Great Hall.

The Queen herself stood waiting for them.

'Peter, welcome to Elmar,' she said warmly as she grasped his hands. Aged though she was, she stood unaided and Peter saw that her serene grey eyes had lost none of their power. He bowed his head before her.

'Thank you, your majesty,' he said.

'Come now, the King awaits you. We are eager to hear your news, though doubtless you have already told it to Alena,' said the Queen. 'However, we shall not forget our hospitality. First, you must wash and change, for I see that your ride has been long and hard. We will see you at supper.'

So it was that spruced up and feeling much refreshed, Peter joined the King and Queen, together with the princess, at the meal table. He was ravenous, but knew he must answer their questions while he ate.

'Tell me of our son,' said the Queen. 'What news do you have? We have worried about his safety for many a moon now.'

Peter explained all that he had seen and learned. The King winced when he heard about Oswain's broken leg.

'Something must be done about that Earth-Trog,' he said. 'It has become more than just a nuisance. It is a positive menace. As for those Boribars, they shall be routed from the kingdom!'

'Nevertheless, we are overjoyed that Loriana is on her way to assist him,' said the Queen. 'Do continue, Peter.'

All their faces looked grave as Peter told of the tragedy of the Great Forest and of Feldrog's imminent invasion.

'Why, O why, do folk doubt the ways of Elmesh?' exclaimed the King. 'Of course matters are sometimes difficult, but that is no reason to give up. Why did they not simply trust and remain loyal?'

'Subtle are the ways of evil,' said the Queen. 'The wise never forget that.'

It was a long tale for Peter to tell and by the time the King and Queen had finished questioning him, he was exhausted.

'You must rest now,' said the Queen, seeing him stifle a yawn. 'There is nothing more that can be done today.'

'You have done well, my boy,' said the King. 'Very well indeed.' He patted Peter on the shoulder as he rose. 'I wish to thank you for everything.'

'You must be worried about your brother,' said the Queen as they departed from the dining table. 'But do not give up hope. Elmesh is to be trusted, even when things are dark – perhaps even more so then.' She gave him a kindly smile. 'Let us see what tomorrow will bring.'

Peter fell asleep the moment his head touched the pillow. A great weight of responsibility had fallen from his shoulders. He had made it to Elmar. Others would know what to do now. All he hoped was that it would turn out all right in the end.

* * *

The next day dawned bright and clear, though the wind was fresh. After breakfast, Peter met Princess Alena and they talked together on a balcony.

'What do you think will happen?' he asked. 'I can't see how anyone can stop Feldrog between the Great Forest and here.'

'We will have to wait and see. We can make no decisions until Surin and the others arrive,' Alena replied. 'Then we shall have a council of war.'

'If only Oswain were here,' Peter sighed. 'I wonder how he's doing. Let's hope Loriana found him all right.' He was suddenly anxious. 'Supposing I gave her the wrong directions? What then?'

Princess Alena laughed.

'Peter, once she knew that he was alive and you told her where to look, she would make no mistake. Never fear. Love always finds a way!'

Peter sighed again. 'I suppose I'm worried about Andrew too. He must be having a terrible time. If only I hadn't fallen off that wheelbarrow.'

Alena placed her hand on his arm.

'Peter, if you had stayed with Andrew you would both have been prisoners and you would never have found Oswain. We simply must believe that Elmesh is somehow in control of all that is happening.' She looked him in the eyes. 'I know Andrew will be all right. I just know it, even though it's hard to believe. Just hold on.'

Peter nodded glumly and agreed as best he could.

17

Plans Are Laid

At midday a runner came to report that Surin had entered Elmar with a sizeable troop. Peter met him at lunch.

'So you arrived in good shape, Peter,' said Surin as soon as he spotted him. 'No further mishaps? Good. I expect Trotter and your sister to arrive with Karador later this afternoon.'

The council was called together after lunch. It met in the Great Chamber, a beautifully arched room with a circle of magnificently carved wooden chairs. Present were the King and Queen, the Lord Chamberlain and the many nobles of Elmar. Surin attended with his chief captains and advisers. Peter felt overawed by the company and was glad that Alena chose to sit next to him.

'I shouldn't really be here,' he whispered.

'Nonsense,' she replied. 'You are just as important as everyone else.'

King Argil opened the discussions.

'We must protect Elmar and all our peoples. That is our prime duty,' he said. 'I do not believe we should evacuate the city and be scattered. Even if we fled to Traun it would only be a matter of time before Feldrog turned his attention there.'

'I agree,' said Surin. 'We must stop him here. I say this not for the protection of my kingdom, but for freedom itself. We might buy time by fleeing but I for one would not wish for that at the cost of Elmar. We must stand together and fight, or all is lost to this tyrant who considers himself to be a god. Well, let him find out that he is not!'

Everyone present muttered their agreement.

Queen Talesanna spoke. 'Brave words, Surin, and I believe you are right, but let us not underestimate the foe. All other kingdoms have fallen to him with scarcely any resistance. It will not be easy to defeat the one who wields the most potent power of all – the power of fear.'

'Nor, sire, should we forget his army,' spoke up one of Surin's commanders. 'I do not fear to fight and I would rather die than retreat, but let us be well prepared.'

Surin nodded his acceptance of the point.

'There is one here who has had sight of Feldrog and his army,' said King Argil. 'Peter, address us now and tell us what you know.'

Peter gave a start at the mention of his name. He rose to his feet and, stammering a little, said, 'Well, I-I didn't see all that much because I was being chased by Etins. Those are giants, by the way – real giants. Anyway, his army seemed to go on for ever. There must be hundreds and thousands of them.'

The commanders quizzed Peter a little more but he had told them all he could.

'We shall need skill, a careful plan,' suggested the Lord Chamberlain. 'Sheer force against force will not work.'

'We must also find a way of dealing with those giants,' added one of the nobles.

'Before all that, we must secure the city and its inhabitants,' the King insisted. 'Bid all those in the surrounding countryside, all who live in the towns and villages, to come into Elmar. We will provide from the royal purse all that is needed to feed and shelter them. Set guards on the gates and send watchmen onto the road to report what is happening. But don't allow them to stray too close to the enemy.'

While the King's instructions were put into effect, the discussions continued into the afternoon. Messengers came and went, fresh orders were given, further plans were laid. Then came the news that chariots were racing towards the city.

'That will be Karador,' said Surin. 'Perhaps he brings news. Come, Peter, we shall meet them together. You will wish to see your sister, no doubt.'

Karador rode at the head of a large posse of chariots. They swept through the city gates like an express train and came to a breathless halt at the foot of the palace steps. Karador leapt from his chariot and raced up to greet Surin.

'The rest of the army will arrive by nightfall,' he panted. 'I have here all the forest-folk who escaped with Trotter. They are tired and some are a little confused by the haste of our journey, but they are all safe.'

Peter watched as Trotter was assisted from a chariot and into a chair. Two liveried palace grooms carried him up the steps. He still clutched the ancient Book of Truth in his paws. Peter ran across to him.

The badger's face did not break into a smile when he saw his friend. Instead, he looked very haggard and weary.

'Trotter, you made it!' cried Peter, not noticing anything amiss. 'Wasn't it great that I met Surin and he was able to help? I bet you were surprised when Karador and his mob turned up. Brilliant, eh? Anyway, see you soon. I want to find Sarah.'

Trotter held up a feeble paw but Peter was off at once, running among the chariots looking for his sister. Dozens upon dozens of animals milled around and he saw Fumble, Mumble and Grumble and even old Stiggle trying to make sense of it all.

Then there was the Brown family's pet dog from his own world.

'Tatters! I never expected to see you here,' he exclaimed.

'Well, I must have gone barking up the *right* tree!' Tatters answered. 'That's all I did, bark at a tree, and then the next moment I was 'ere. Bloomin' marvellous!'

Peter agreed, but delighted as he was to see Tatters, he still wanted to find his sister.

But to Peter's consternation he couldn't see Sarah anywhere. Gradually, as the animals dispersed to their quarters, it became clear that she wasn't there. He turned to face Trotter, who remained seated at the top of the steps. Surin stood next to him.

Filled with apprehension Peter approached them.

'What's happened, Trotter?' he asked gravely.

'Where's Sarah? She was supposed to be with you. Where is she?'

Trotter raised a weary paw to his face.

'I don't know, Peter,' he croaked. 'We left as you saw and I assumed she was with the rest at the back. It was only after some hours, when I felt that everyone needed a rest, that I discovered her missing. I wasn't sure what to do. Several offered to return, but then the weather broke and we had to shelter from a storm. After that, I knew it would be foolish to return.' He gazed sadly at Peter. 'I'm sorry.'

Peter was silent and he bit his lip. 'You know what she's done, don't you?' he said at last.

Trotter nodded slowly. 'It was not difficult to work out,' he said.

'She's gone back for Andrew.' Peter clenched his fists, suddenly restless with frustration. 'That means he's got my brother *and* my sister,' he fumed. 'What am I going to do? I must go and help them.'

Surin interrupted him. He placed a firm hand on Peter's shoulder. 'That will do no good,' he said. 'All it would mean is that all three of you would be prisoners. No, Peter, you must learn in the battles of life to keep yourself in control. Those who act on impulse often prove to be only foolish heroes. True heroes carefully count the cost and then take the risk to help others.'

Slowly Peter calmed down, but it wasn't easy.

'I want to get that Feldrog,' he said. 'What are we going to do then?'

'That is what we must now discuss,' said Surin. 'It is

one thing to defend the city, but even Elmar cannot expect to hold out for ever. At some point we will have to make a fight of it. That will be your opportunity to be a hero, believe me.'

They entered the palace together. Trotter was greeted with great honour by all concerned and was given a seat by the Queen's right hand.

Discussions continued until supper time. Then servants brought food and drink for the assembly.

'It marks the end, you know,' said Trotter to the Queen.

She eyed him with a strange look.

'Tell me more,' she insisted.

'It is prophesied in *The Tale of the Seven Rainbows*. This is the passing of the age, and the end of all things as we know them,' he said.

She was about to reply when there was a commotion at the door. A runner came stumbling in. He bowed hastily before the King, who was in the middle of a mouthful of food.

'I beg your pardon, your majesty, but I bring you urgent news. Something awful is coming along the road. I've just seen a terrible light, and it's almost upon us!'

Surin was the first to the door. Peter and Princess Alena followed right behind.

'What foul sorcery is this?' Surin growled as he strode across the courtyard and ran briskly up the nearest flight of stone stairs. 'It is not possible that Feldrog could be here so soon.'

The top of the steps opened onto a balcony and

revealed a door leading into one of the turrets. Surin pushed it open and bounded up the winding staircase within. It was all Peter and Alena could do to keep up with him. He appeared quite unaware of their presence.

They emerged from another door onto a high battlement. From this giddy height it was possible to see over the entire city and, beyond its walls, to the surrounding countryside. The last blush of sunset still tinged the western sky and glinted faintly off the darkening surface of the River Til. Down below, lamps lit many a window, and a hazy dusk bathed the entire city. But it was to the East that Surin's eyes turned.

An upright bobbin of spinning light, flashing pink, blue, green and orange, was rapidly approaching the city through the air, high above the Eastern Road. Mesmerised by the sight and wondering what it foreboded, the three observers watched as it passed over the city wall and glided straight towards the palace.

'Quickly! Down the stairs,' cried Surin, now noticing that Peter and Alena were with him. 'It's going to strike the entrance to the Great Hall.'

Without further ado, all three raced down the winding staircase. Leaping and stumbling they burst through the door at the foot of the turret and tumbled onto the balcony. Surin had his sword at the ready.

By now the bobbin of light was whirling above the courtyard and in front of the entrance to the Great Hall. Eyes peered from every window and the whole city had come to a standstill to gaze in awe at the sight. Surin, Peter and Alena were thunderstruck, for even as they looked two fiery wings began to sprout from the centre of the light.

Slowly, the spinning stopped and the light took the form of an enormous butterfly made up of a myriad twinkling stars. Nestling between the wings were two figures: a man and a woman.

'It's Oswain!' shouted Peter.

'And Loriana!' added Alena.

Surin sheathed his sword with a sigh. 'Of all the crazy ways to arrive! They might have warned us! We can do without false alarms at the moment.'

Gently, the butterfly descended to the courtyard floor and Oswain stepped from his glittering conveyance. The Ice Maiden took his proffered hand and alighted gracefully. At this, a great cheer rose from the assembled onlookers as they too recognised the travellers. The wings closed and with a faint tinkling sound the butterfly changed into a cluster of spangled light that rose and settled in a halo around the highest point of the palace dome.

'Come on!' cried Peter. 'Let's get down there and say hello.'

By the time they reached the courtyard, King Argil and Queen Talesanna had emerged from the chamber and were already talking with the couple.

'We thought you were lost to us for ever,' whispered the Queen. Her eyes were moist.

'Welcome back, son,' said the King. 'And you too, my dear Loriana.'

'It is good to be back, Father,' Oswain replied. 'There

were times when I despaired of ever seeing any of you again. But, Elmesh be praised, here we are.'

'And none too soon, either,' replied the King. 'We need your counsel and leadership as never before.'

Oswain glanced at Loriana. 'Then we must waste no time telling of our adventures,' he said.

'There is, I think, little that we do not know already,' said the Queen with a smile. 'Peter is here. He is quite a hero.'

'He is indeed,' Oswain answered warmly. 'Without his courage all would be lost by now. Where is he?'

He glanced around until his eyes rested on Peter among the small crowd of onlookers. Surin ushered him forward.

Oswain greeted him warmly and then addressed the assembled people.

'This young lad is a worthy knight of the realm. Let him be honoured for his bravery and good sense in the midst of great danger. I owe my life to him.'

To Peter's great embarrassment everyone began to applaud and to cheer him. Princess Alena came forward and both she and the Ice Maiden kissed him.

'It wasn't really anything,' he blurted. 'I just did what I could. We were too late to save the Great Forest, though. I feel terrible about that. Really I do.'

Oswain placed a hand on his shoulder.

'Don't worry about that, Peter. Grievous though it is, all is not yet lost. We must still hope in Elmesh.' He laughed. 'Remember, things are not as dark as in the Boribars' wagon!'

He turned then and properly greeted his adopted sister, Princess Alena. Then he spotted Surin.

'My friend!' he cried. 'So you came. I am grateful that you should risk your kingdom to help us.'

'We are all at risk,' replied Surin. 'It is the least I can do. I have long since learned that we who serve Elmesh must stick together in times of trouble.'

'Nevertheless, it shall not be forgotten,' Oswain replied.

With that, the royal party entered the Great Hall.

In spite of the dangers that threatened the city, the evening was filled with great rejoicing at Oswain's homecoming. Many friends were greeted. All necessary news was exchanged and it was unanimously agreed that Oswain should act as commander-in-chief of the army.

Late that evening, he addressed the entire assembly in the Council Chamber.

'Feldrog draws ever nearer,' he said. 'Now that he is on the road from the Great Forest to Elmar there is small chance of delay. Tomorrow will be the fateful day, for I judge that he will reach the city by late afternoon. It gives us little time to prepare ourselves for battle. Indeed, it would be folly to attempt meeting his vast army in the field. Our first action must be to close the city gates and to secure ourselves against siege.'

'I don't much like being cooped up, and nor will my generals,' Surin growled. 'However, I agree with you, Oswain. Let us only hope that it will not be long before we find a way to repel the invader.'

'You and I should speak together, Surin,' Oswain answered. 'Meanwhile, I suggest that everyone else should get what sleep they can. Tomorrow will be a long day.'

There was one who did not leave the chamber.

Trotter, seated quietly in the background, waited until everyone else had departed.

'I could not come out to greet you,' he said. 'Alas, I am weary. Also, I am ashamed, for I have failed in my charge. I could not contain the rebellion. At my feet must lie the blame for the loss of your kingdom.'

Oswain looked with kindness on the frail old badger. There were tears in his eyes.

'Do not blame yourself for what you could not prevent, my friend,' he said. 'You did not doubt, nor did you surrender to treachery. Such loyalty is of more value to me than a whole kingdom.'

Oswain's words comforted Trotter, and when he fell asleep where he sat, his face was at last peaceful.

18

Surrounded!

Dawn broke cold and bleak, and so began the fateful long wait. A chill wind blew from the East. A fitting sign of what was to come, Oswain thought.

His leg had almost fully recovered thanks to the Ice Maiden's healing powers and he strode about the palace with only the slightest limp to betray his former injuries. He had much to organise.

At midday the last of the runners came back into the shelter of the city with the news that Feldrog was almost within sight. On hearing this, Oswain ordered the gates to be closed and barricaded.

Oswain ascended the battlements above the main gates. King Argil and Queen Talesanna, Lord Trotter, Princess Alena, Surin, Karador and Peter accompanied him. Heavily armed soldiers from the combined armies lined the entire circumference of the wall. Everyone else was ordered to shelter in their homes.

At last, the awesome spectacle of Feldrog's chariot came into view. Behind him stretched the seemingly endless columns of his army. Huge Etins stomped alongside.

'This is it,' said Oswain, and he braced himself.

The chariot-throne came to a halt at some distance

from the city and those watching wondered what Feldrog was doing. It soon became clear. Under the direction of his commanders, the army began steadily to encircle the city. The process took hours and when it was completed the great walls were surrounded by a countless host of warriors. Only the area around the main gate remained unoccupied.

The chariot-throne began to advance. Soon it was obvious that the main gate had been left clear for Feldrog himself.

Peter peered in vain to try to distinguish Andrew or Sarah among the toiling children, but he could not make them out. He hoped they were not already dead.

A line of heralds accompanied the chariot and, once it had come to rest, they advanced and stood in front of the children. They placed golden trumpets to their lips and played a loud fanfare. Feldrog rose slowly from his throne.

'Hail to the Ruler of the Empires of the World, Master of the Universe, Eternal Glory. Bow your knees in unworthy homage to your Lord!' cried a herald.

Those on the wall remained unmoved.

Then Feldrog himself spoke.

'I come to you as the Prince of Peace,' he cried. 'Bend yourselves to my eternal majesty, surrender your city and your kingdom, and there will be no bloodshed. My armies will secure the territory and you will be permitted to be servants in my everlasting empire. By my grace I grant you the freedom to worship me as your supreme Lord.'

Oswain spoke out on behalf of the royal party.

'Your offer is rejected, Feldrog. We have no need to grant it consideration, for we serve and worship Elmesh alone. You speak blasphemous rubbish in your arrogance. How dare you claim such noble titles in the name of evil!'

'You are foolish and insolent, Oswain, king without a kingdom! Great rulers in your own eyes you may be, but you underestimate my power. Do you not know that I am invincible? No kingdom in the world has successfully resisted me,' Feldrog answered.

'There's got to be a first time,' Peter breathed to Alena.

'Your arrogance does you no credit,' cried Surin.

'Ah, foolish Surin of Traun. Do you think all my army is here? Even now your kingdom topples and my forces surround your citadel. As soon as Elmar bows I shall conduct myself thence and claim your crown also!'

Surin blanched at this news.

'My grace and patience are at an end!' cried Feldrog.

He stretched forth his needle-like sceptre, pointing it first to the left and then to the right of Oswain's band. Immediately, all the soldiers on the walls began to cry out in pain and fear. Their groans echoed around the city perimeter as they fell to their knees, begging for mercy. Many cried that they would serve Feldrog for ever, if only he would permit them.

'Did I not say he was the Lord of fear?' muttered the Ice Maiden.

'Your army is defeated. It is all over,' Feldrog stated.

'All around your city they are on their knees begging for the honour of worshipping me. Now do you understand?'

'Worship that is forced is no worship,' Oswain declared. 'Nothing is changed. We do not surrender.'

Then Feldrog pointed the Sting at the company. At once, Peter cried out in pain. Princess Alena followed suit. The faces of the others were set in taut masks of agony.

'No!' Oswain cried. 'Never!'

Standing almost beside Feldrog on the chariot and petrified with fear, Sarah fought with despair. When first she had spotted Oswain and all the others alive and well, her heart had leapt. Now she saw that they were powerless against the tyrant, and they had not even recognised her.

Yet even as she beheld the anguish of her friends, the little spark of hope that she had cherished in the deepest part of her being began to burn anew. She could still choose to die for others. Feldrog had not taken that away.

Suddenly, she turned. Fighting the overwhelming fear and despair that she felt, Sarah seized Feldrog's Sting. It burned in her hand like a red-hot poker. She gasped in pain and recoiled, clutching her hand in agony.

With a snarl of outrage Feldrog threw her off like a rag doll. She stumbled back and lost her footing. With a cry of alarm she teetered on the brink of the dais and then fell to the jewel-laden floor of the chariot and struck it with a hiss of diamonds.

Without doubt, these broke her fall and saved her from death or serious injury.

Feldrog had not finished with her, however. Lying on her back she faced his towering form high above her. His face was the colour of thunder and with a cold sneer he pointed the Sting straight at her body. She writhed in pain as dread seized her heart in its vicelike grip.

'Help me! Someone help me!' she cried.

While this was taking place, the children who pulled the chariot stood watching. Every one of them was frozen with fear. Yet as Feldrog concentrated his spite on Sarah, something wavered and then broke. Andrew found unexpected strength return. He no longer looked with stark horror at his sister's plight. He had to act.

Rushing forward before the overseers or anyone else could stop him, he clambered onto the chariot and struggled through the sea of diamonds towards Sarah. Wildly he began to grab handfuls of the precious stones and throw them with all his might at Feldrog.

One of them must have struck the tyrant in the face, for Feldrog lowered his wand in order to wipe his eye. It was Andrew's chance. He seized Sarah's hand and dragged her to her feet.

'Come on, sis,' he gasped. 'Come on!'

The other children continued to watch the events with trepidation. Then, unexpectedly, one of them broke from the crowd and shinned up onto the chariot. Wading through the diamonds, he made straight for the stairs and, pushing past the bemused dancing girls, rushed up onto the dais. Without stopping, he thudded hard into Feldrog.

'Gumboil!' exclaimed Andrew, as he saw who it was.

The unexpected impact of Gumboil's tubby form was sufficient to throw Feldrog completely off balance. He fell to the floor of the dais, and as he did so struck his head on the arm of his throne. With a groan, the tyrant passed out. Sting slipped from his grasp and rolled off the dais onto the diamonds below.

At once the fear lifted. Sarah staggered to the edge of the chariot and, with Andrew's help, clambered to the ground. Gumboil tumbled down the stairs and joined them.

'Quick now. Run for it. All of you,' yelled Andrew. 'Make for the gates. They'll help us.'

Loosed from their bondage, the children needed no further encouragement. With loud cries they raced towards the gates.

Perched on the battlements, Oswain's band watched these events in amazement.

'Good old Sarah! Well done, Andrew!' Peter shouted. 'Hurrah!'

Everything had happened so quickly that even the overseers were stunned. Open-mouthed, they gazed at their fallen master. However, as the children began to run for the shelter of the city, they gave chase.

Oswain was quick to spot the danger.

'Get the postern gate open and let them in,' he commanded. 'As fast as you can.'

Then two of the overseers cried out and fell to the ground, both of them brought down by lethal crossbow bolts. Two others died in quick succession. It was enough to cause the rest to waver and it increased the children's chances of making good their escape.

The next moment two stocky figures armed with crossbows came running to the children's aid.

'It's Dringol and Brankleshanks!' cried Peter from the battlements.

The two Dweorgs continued to hold the overseers at bay while the children fled for the safety of the city.

But then soldiers from the fringes of Feldrog's army began to join in the chase. It was going to be too much for the two Dweorgs.

Suddenly, the Ice Maiden cried in a loud voice. *'Naida, hasto carenna tomo tocrata!'*

At once, the Naida that hovered around the palace dome swooped down towards the children. At the Ice Maiden's command they formed a circle of protection around them and the Dweorgs. Many of the pursuers dropped back in wonder at this. Others who continued the chase simply buckled at the knees and fell instantly into a deep sleep.

Within a few moments, the children were pouring into the city through the small postern gate. As soon as they were all inside it was hastily re-barricaded. Everyone was delighted.

Sarah and Andrew, together with Gumboil, were sent for straight away. Gasping with relief, they ran up the steps onto the battlements and fell into the welcoming embrace of their friends. By now all the soldiers on the wall had recovered and a great cheer arose that echoed and re-echoed across the city.

In the midst of all this rejoicing, Andrew turned to Gumboil.

'Why did you do it?' he asked.

Gumboil looked a little abashed.

'I dunno, really,' he said. 'I've been selfish all my life, I suppose. It . . . it was just seeing that you had the guts to help, really. I suddenly wanted to do something, even just one thing, to help someone else.'

'Well, you certainly did,' said Andrew with feeling. 'I reckon you saved our lives.'

'It is fair to say that you saved all of us,' said Oswain. He faced the three children. 'I don't know what would have happened otherwise. You are heroes, every one of you.'

The Ice Maiden looked with concern at Sarah's hand.

'That was a very brave thing you did,' she murmured. 'But that is just like you, Sarah.'

'I wasn't brave, really,' she replied. 'I suppose I thought that it was better to die than to give in to him.' She winced as the Ice Maiden bathed the burn.

'It will heal,' Loriana pronounced. 'You have too much love in you for the sting of fear to do you permanent harm.'

'As for you two, that was really unexpected,' exclaimed Oswain addressing Dringol and Brankleshanks.

'Are we not Dweorgs of the Oath?'* said Dringol.

'We are your servants for life,' added his brother, Brankleshanks.

---

*You can read all about this in *Oswain and the Mystery of the Star Stone*.

Oswain bowed to their honour.

Attention turned back to Feldrog. Anxious advisers were tending to him, but the Sting still lay among the diamonds. No one would dare touch that.

'We have very little time before he tries again,' Surin observed.

'Then get the troops off the walls,' said Oswain. 'They will be safer out of sight.'

'What will we do?' Loriana asked Oswain. 'His power is immense. Although we may resist for some long while, our people cannot. It is surely only a matter of time before the army overruns us.'

Oswain shook his head. 'We will find a way, if there is one. However, we must be quick about it. Look, he is recovering!'

Sure enough, Feldrog was back on his throne and gazing around him. Moments later, he rose and began shakily to descend the steps to retrieve the Sting.

Those on the wall watched with growing apprehension and wondered what would happen next.

19

Revenge of the Earth-Trog

They did not have to wait long. At the very instant Feldrog's hand touched his sceptre, there was a deep rumble. Immediately, the ground began to quake with a terrible violence. Buildings shook and the city walls trembled to their very foundations.

'What now?' Surin muttered grimly.

The answer to his question soon became terrifyingly clear.

A million marching men cause a lot of vibration. Deep below the Waste Plains to the east of the Great Forest, an ancient evil was roused once more. Stirred by the steady tramp of Feldrog's mighty army, irresistibly attracted by the insistent beat of those footsteps, the Earth-Trog had journeyed, seeking and hungering, through the deep, dark paths of the earth. Its search brought it to Elmar, just as Feldrog arrived with his troops.

The Earth-Trog wanted blood. Lots of it. Nothing excited it more than the prospect of thousands upon thousands of living beings falling into its jaws. With mindless malice, it thought on the waiting feast, and the more it thought, the greater in size it grew. By the time it reached the city of Elmar it was immense, and its greedy trembling tentacles reached out in all directions.

There was a whole army to be swallowed up!

Yet while it delved secretly beneath the unsuspecting army, the Earth-Trog sensed something else besides the feast that awaited it. Old foes were nearby; people and animals who had denied the beast its prey in times past. The bearer of a terrible light that had once seared its cold heart with white-hot fire was there too. The Earth-Trog could feel it and was enraged. Filled with primeval spite, it suddenly wanted nothing more than to destroy and devour those it hated. Even Feldrog's army could wait while it did so.

Tunnelling furiously through the ground, the Earth-Trog began to tear angrily at the very roots of the city.

The first anyone knew of this was when the earth started to tremble beneath their feet. Moments later, huge cracks yawned in the mighty walls of the city. Stones fell in noisy avalanches. Towers and battlements crumbled in dusty ruins. The oak gates splintered like matchwood. Everywhere, people fled for their lives.

Yet there was no safety within the city. Roofs started to cave in. Houses tossed and tipped like ships in a storm as the heaving ground split asunder. Even the palace was not immune. With a horrendous crash the roof of the Great Hall fell. It was followed by the collapse of the Tower of Visions. In minutes the beautiful building lay in ruins. People stared in awe as a huge chasm opened to swallow the waters of the River Til.

Thrown to and fro, the terrified population of the city ran for the open spaces and prayed for deliverance.

Strangely, the one part of the wall to remain standing

was the battlement above the main gate where Oswain and his companions stood. Helpless and amazed, they stared in anguish at the destruction of the city. Had they really underestimated Feldrog's powers?

There was little time to think. The ground between Feldrog's chariot and the main gate erupted with a terrible tearing sound. A monstrous malevolent head of stinking brown slime burst from the earth and reared above the battlements like a dark tidal wave. One word roared from its shapeless bulk: 'Vengeance!'

It was all Oswain and his friends could do to remain upright and they feared the battlement would crumble at any moment. Sarah screamed in horror and clutched at the Ice Maiden. Even she blanched at the sight.

'Elmesh, spare us!' she whispered.

'It's the Earth-Trog!' gasped Peter. 'We're done for!'

The Earth-Trog appeared to savour the moment. It towered above the trapped company, blotting out all sight of the sky as its shadow fell across them. How it would enjoy engulfing its enemies and crushing them to death!

Princess Alena was the first to gather her wits. Memory of a past encounter with the Earth-Trog flashed into her mind. Desperately, she fumbled in her dress. Even as the monster reared its body in readiness to crash down upon its prey, she drew out the one thing she thought might save them. It was the famed Star-Stone of Elmar and Alena's own birthstone. Heedless of her own safety, she staggered across the heaving stones and fearlessly stared into the slimy face of the monster.

'In the name of Elmesh, draw back!' she cried.

The Star-Stone instantly glowed like a blob of white-hot metal. Those around the Princess had to shield their eyes from the glare and the Earth-Trog wavered before its terrifying light. It was time enough for the Ice Maiden to call for the Naida.

At once, a glittering ball of spangled light formed between the company and their attacker. The air filled with a high ringing sound. It was too much for the Earth-Trog. With a roar of rage and frustration it recoiled and swiftly slid defeated back into the ground.

'Brilliant!' cried Andrew.

'That was well done, Alena,' said the Queen with a gasp of relief. 'Few would have thought what to do at such a moment.'

The Princess smiled.

'I learned it from Peter a long time ago,' she said. She grinned in his direction.

'It was a good job you did,' said Andrew with feeling. 'I thought we'd had it just then.'

'It was certainly close,' Oswain agreed. 'Excellently done, Alena.'

Everyone took it in turns to hug the Princess.

King Argil looked back at Elmar. His face was glum.

'The city is ruined beyond repair, though. I did not wish to live long enough to see such a day,' he groaned.

'Do not speak like that, Father,' said Oswain. 'We are not finished yet.'

'Nor are we finished with Feldrog. Look!' growled Surin. He pointed in the direction of the tyrant's chariot.

Feldrog had watched in amazement as the Earth-Trog wrecked the city of Elmar. Truly the tyrant possessed powers beyond even his own imagining, he decided! There was, of course, the loss of all the wealth and splendour of the city, but that was a trifle compared to conquering the great kingdom of the West. Resistance was broken. The realm was his for the taking, and that was what mattered. With a word of command, he ushered his Etins forward.

The lumbering giants advanced on all sides and began at once to remove the wreckage of the walls to make clear paths so that Feldrog's army could invade the city. There was nothing anyone could do to stop them. The few arrows and spears thrown by the loyal troops of Elmar simply bounced off the monsters like paper darts. Most people fled.

'What are we going to do?' Sarah wailed.

They heard Feldrog's voice again.

'You have tasted a little of the power at my disposal,' he cried. 'Such a fate awaits all those who dare to insult my glorious name. I gave you the opportunity to surrender willingly. That time is now past and my patience is exhausted. Death awaits you and all your people. I shall spare nobody. Even your very names shall be wiped from history so that you are remembered no more!'

'You're a fool if you think the Earth-Trog obeys you,' shouted Surin. 'Your arrogance does not frighten us, and nor will we be defeated that easily.'

'Brave words! But your last,' returned Feldrog. He raised his terrible sceptre. 'I call on the Lord of Darkness to serve me. To him I dedicate this kingdom.'

At once the generals began to shout orders, which were passed around the circumference of the city. With a mighty roar and a clash of steel, the army began to close in on all sides. The noose tightened as a million men surged inwards.

'This is it,' said Oswain grimly. He unsheathed his sword and prepared to defend the remains of the steps leading up to the battlements. Surin and Karador did likewise.

Yet it was not destined that the vast army of Feldrog should breach the ruined walls of Elmar. Before ever a soldier set foot upon the rubble, the ground trembled once more – this time even more violently than before. The Earth-Trog had not finished. Deprived of its first prey, its mindless insatiable hunger turned now to the advancing troops. They would still make a good meal!

A loud splitting sound went up, and a huge chasm began to tear open right around the perimeter of the city. The remains of the walls fell sliding and crashing into its depths. Roaring with indignation, the Etins struggled to escape, but to no avail. The chasm was too wide even for the giants. Struggling to the end, each one tumbled to his doom.

Feldrog's army fell into disarray. Such was its vast size that those at the rear were still pushing forward, while troops at the front desperately sought to flee from the awful ever-widening chasm. Panic took over. The generals lost control and in the chaos thousands upon thousands were driven into the cruel jaws of the Earth-

Trog. Feldrog rose from his throne and stared in frustrated rage at the carnage.

As for those on the battlement, their immediate relief turned to silent horror as they watched the destruction of Feldrog's men.

'What a waste of life,' Oswain groaned. He turned away in disgust.

By the time it had finished a deep gorge a hundred metres wide encompassed the entire city and the Earth-Trog had devoured almost everyone in Feldrog's vast army. Those who did escape fled for their lives. Even Feldrog did not frighten them as much as the monster beneath the ground.

Gradually things quietened down. The Earth-Trog was satisfied, at least for the present. Only the occasional rumble betrayed its continued presence. Slowly, the tattered remains of Feldrog's army, mostly his officers, crept back and gathered around him. His chariot-throne seemed to be the only safe place.

A yawning abyss now separated the troops from the city. No one could come out, and no one could go in. It was stalemate. Citizens of Elmar began to gather behind what remained of the main gate. The King and Queen greeted them from the battlements with solemn waves. Everybody waited in silence for the Earth-Trog's next move. It had thwarted everyone.

A tense hour passed. Conferences took place on both sides. Plans were laid. Time seemed to stand still and the stench of death hung over the city. Then slowly, seeping up like a poisonous mist, a curtain of darkness began to arise from the depths of the canyon. Higher and higher it rose until soon it hung like a black veil, stretching into the evening sky and completely enclosing the city. Everything beyond the ruined walls of Elmar was blotted out, so that the city became like an island in the midst of a sea of endless, silent blackness.

Horror fell upon all the people of the city. Children and babies cried, women wailed, men groaned. On the ruined battlements, only a few metres from the dark veil, Oswain's company stood their ground as best they could. Trembling with fear, Sarah clung to the Ice Maiden, while Peter and Andrew stayed close to Oswain. Princess Alena and her real father, Surin, held hands tightly. Trotter, holding his book, stared steadfastly into the blackness. They remembered now: Feldrog had called upon the Lord of Darkness himself.

Then the silent accusations began.

Every failure, every mistake that any one of them had ever made came vividly to their minds. The words screamed out, 'Guilty! Guilty! Guilty!' Heads bowed in shame and despair; hearts quailed at the judgement. Hell awaited. Faces appeared in the darkness; evil mocking visions of distorted monsters whirled and wove through the black veil, with wild wailings that drove people half-mad with terror. Many grovelled on the ground with their hands over their ears, trying in vain to shut out the awful noise. Others struck their own heads like mad things.

Peter, Sarah and Andrew stared aghast at one another. They had been pretty rotten to each other on occasions.

There could be no forgiveness, no hope. It was too late for tears. They were separated from one another for ever and damned to eternal torment.

'Elmesh have mercy upon us,' gasped Oswain.

A tunnel seemed to open before his eyes. He felt himself walking through a wasted wind-torn valley. Dark clouds threatened on all sides. His bleak path narrowed and soon he walked a rocky knife-edge that fell away in a steep precipice on either side. He dare not look down. His steps faltered. Unknown tendrils snaked from the abyss and sought to entangle his legs.

He knew he must not fall. How hard for a leader not to lose his nerve!

'I will not be afraid. Elmesh . . . Elmesh is with me, though I do not see him,' he whispered. 'He will lead me through.'

A faint light appeared ahead. He fixed his eyes upon it and pressed steadfastly on. The path widened and suddenly he was back on the battlement with his companions. A cold sweat sheened his ashen face. He stared at Alena. Her Star-Stone gave a pale flicker. Was this the light he had seen, he wondered? Overhead, the Naida continued to hover, but their light was muted. Even the Ice Maiden looked pale.

He faced the dark veil once more.

Only then did he spot the tiny point of light. It was high in the black mist.

'Look!' he gasped. 'Up there.'

He pointed with his finger and the others followed his gaze.

'Elrilion! It is Elrilion,' cried the Ice Maiden. 'See, the star of Elmesh shines even in this hellish darkness. Renew your hope, my friends!'

The light grew steadily stronger. At first it seemed no more than a pin-prick in the shroud, but before long the darkness began to part and the skies became visible to the grateful eyes of the watchers. By now it was night time, but it seemed like daylight compared to the awful darkness of the pit. The heavens shone with a million starry diamonds and the air was again clean and clear. Elrilion had risen and its limpid beauty radiated hope into the hearts of the onlookers. Everyone heaved a sigh of relief. Back on the ground in the city there was laughter. People began to talk. Arms were thrown around one another to comfort and to cheer.

Oswain had just begun to think again about Feldrog when Loriana caught his arm.

'Oswain, look!' she said in a hushed voice. She directed his gaze heavenward.

For a moment he couldn't believe his eyes. He blinked and looked again. There was no doubt about it. The stars were moving! This was the day to end all days, that was for sure.

It wasn't long before the entire population realised what was happening. Everywhere, fingers pointed to the heavens as people babbled excitedly about the meaning of this latest phenomenon.

'That is certainly not Feldrog's doing,' murmured the Ice Maiden.

For the next hour, they watched as the stars slowly

spiralled into one great cosmic swirl, leaving behind an empty blackness where only moments before there had been bright light. It was a dizzying sight and many of the onlookers clung to one another for support. If you were not careful you thought the ground was spinning and the stars stationary.

Only Elrilion, the star of Elmesh, remained fixed. It was to this that all the others were being drawn. Within the hour, they formed a milky river that poured steadily into Elrilion until it was the only star left in the heavens. Awe fell upon the watching crowds. Their city was destroyed and cut off from the outside world. A wild monster lurked beneath the ground and a tyrant awaited his moment beyond the chasm. Now the heavens had changed for ever.

'It's moving. Elrilion is moving!' gasped Peter.

Sure enough, the star of Elmesh was shifting. For a few moments, people wondered in alarm if the last star was going to vanish too, and leave them in eternal darkness. Then it became obvious that Elrilion was growing in size. The amazed onlookers realised that it must be rushing towards them at incalculable speed. Fresh anxiety gripped their hearts.

It wasn't long before the star was as large as a full moon and the world was drenched in its silvery-blue light. Yet still it grew bigger until it filled the horizon. The remaining darkness of the pit was utterly extinguished, as with a final faint wail of despair it faded away completely.

Nothing now remained except the people standing

amidst the ruins of Elmar, and Feldrog with the remnants of his army waiting beyond the chasm. The cold light of Elrilion threw long stark shadows across the landscape. It drained all the colours, so that everything stood in silhouette against its silver glare.

With bated breath, the population of Elmar waited to see what would happen next. On the battlements, Trotter spoke.

'It is the end of the world,' he pronounced. 'Just as the Book said it would be!'

20

What Became of Feldrog

Sarah felt herself trembling on the very edge of time. She gazed in wonder at Elrilion. The air was warm and she marvelled that with the star so close they had not been burned to a frazzle. It was all so unlike what she had learned at school.

'What does it all mean?' she whispered. 'What is happening to us?'

'All things change at the end of time,' said the Ice Maiden.

'I just don't understand,' she answered. 'I mean, the Great Forest has gone. I thought the Merestone would protect it, but it didn't. Then, I suppose, I thought Feldrog's army would be defeated by . . . by the Naida, or by Arca and a billion other eagles, like before.' Her bottom lip trembled. 'Where is Arca? I wish he were here.' She gazed at the aged King. 'I'm so sorry that your beautiful city has been ruined by that horrible Earth-Trog. Why did it have to happen?' She waved her hand vaguely at the sky. 'And now this. There's nothing left, and we're still in terrible danger.'

The Ice Maiden placed a comforting arm around Sarah's shoulders.

'You are young, Sarah. Young to understand such

things, but not too young to experience them,' she said wisely. 'Trust in Elmesh. You'll see.'

Trotter coughed and spoke.

'Sarah, do you remember when we were in the Enchanted Glade? We read something from the Book of Truth.'

She nodded. 'Yes, I do remember, but I'm afraid I didn't take too much notice of it. Perhaps I should have.'

'Let me remind you,' said the badger.

He opened the book at a marker and read these words: 'This is the sign of the last day. Dawn will break at midnight, and the end is only the beginning. Dark troubles will swirl like cloudy water, yet from their gloom shall burst fresh light. When fear-shrouded doubters least expect it, new things will spring from the old. Courage! All shall be mended at the coming of the King.'

'Courage! All shall be mended at the coming of the King,' repeated the Ice Maiden.

Sarah pondered the words.

'It all seems true,' she said slowly. 'Although I still feel afraid, and I don't understand which king is meant. We've got three here – Surin, Argil and Oswain.'

A cry from Peter interrupted them.

'Look at Elrilion. There in the centre,' he exclaimed. 'Something's happening.'

All eyes turned to the blazing silver star that by now filled most of the sky. It was difficult to see much because of its brilliance. Yet unmistakably, in the centre of the star, a small sparkling light of even greater brightness was flashing regularly.

'Do you think it's some kind of signal, or a message?' Andrew asked. He wondered if it meant that someone lived on the star, even though that seemed impossible.

Before anyone could answer him, a slender curving beam of glorious sapphire blue shot from the flashing light. It made towards them at a simply incredible speed. As the onlookers stared in wonder, it began to open out into a flat fan of luminous blue crystal that was shot through with vivid flashes of fire. Time and space seemed to shrink before this vast celestial sea and a sense of awe and wonderment fell upon all who watched its approach.

Soon its spread encompassed the entire horizon and still it drew nearer. The glittering diamonds of Feldrog's chariot faded to insignificance and what was once a magnificent array now appeared cheap and tawdry. What remained of his army bowed to the ground in terror. Feldrog, still defiant, stood and waved his sceptre threateningly.

'Fools! Stand to your feet. I am the Supreme Master of the Universe,' he cried. 'You are commanded to worship only me.' But his voice sounded feeble, unimportant.

As the awe-inspiring celestial sea drew ever closer, a sudden wind blew up. It carried with it the fresh tang of salt air that reminded people of seaside holidays. Something further was happening on the surface of Elrilion too. What looked like a cloud of white smoke began to pour from the source of the sapphire beam. Everyone watched in wonder as the cloud grew larger and larger. It was obviously streaming towards them high above the crystal sea. The wind grew stronger. Soon it was a howling gale and people began to cling to one another to avoid being blown over.

Sarah was the first to realise that it was not a cloud, nor smoke, that was coming towards them.

'They're . . . they're eagles!' she gasped. 'Millions and millions of them. Look, you can see their wings. Arca must be coming!' In spite of the wind she jumped for joy and clapped her hands excitedly. Oswain had to grab her to prevent her from being blown off the battlements.

Sure enough, it was possible to make out the shapes of countless white eagles streaming from Elrilion towards where they stood. Peter guessed that it was the beating of their wings that had created the wind. Everyone began to cheer at the coming of the mighty messengers of Elmesh.

Down below, among the inhabitants and refugees in the city of Elmar, William and Mary and Taril and the other members of the Guild of the White Eagle gazed heavenwards, eyes wide with wonder.

'It's all true,' whispered William. 'There really are white eagles, and there's an Arca.'

'Amazing!' whispered Taril. He could feel a lump rising in his throat. Everyone had laughed at the Guild but now he knew that their simple faith and the telling of the old stories was worth it all.

Feldrog's face fell. He clambered swiftly from his throne and tried to shelter behind his chariot along with his cowering cronies. He did not seem so high and mighty any longer and nobody feared him. In fact, hardly anyone took any notice of the once mighty potentate.

However, the wind must have made Feldrog's chariot its special target. It caught the pink canopy behind the throne and tore it to pieces. The vast heaps of diamonds blew away like glittering chaff – a fortune to the wind! Then the wheels collapsed and the whole thing tipped over and broke into smithereens as though it had been made of boxwood.

Andrew cheered with delight as he saw the proud throne toppled.

'Serves him right! Fancy thinking he was some kind of god,' he cried.

Feldrog, once so mighty, now looked pathetic among the splintered remains of his throne. In a last desperate effort he waved his fearsome sceptre at the wind.

'Cease!' he cried. 'I, Feldrog the Almighty, command you!'

But the wind scornfully tore the Sting from his grasp and dashed it to the ground, where it broke into tiny fragments that were instantly blown away. The next moment, Feldrog lost his balance and fell over. Scrabbling desperately, he clung to the earth in an effort not to be blown away himself.

Instead, he began to shrink.

At first, the amazed onlookers could not believe their eyes. Yet sure enough the once all-powerful tyrant was becoming smaller and smaller. The same was happening to his generals, and Sarah saw that Terras and Sorda had not escaped either. Before long they were all no bigger than midgets. Nor did it stop there. Soon, Feldrog and the remnants of his army were reduced to the size of toy soldiers, and after that it was impossible to distinguish them from the dust of the ground.

With a final howl of victory a blast of wind carried them away into oblivion – and that really was the end of Feldrog the Almighty!

By now the celestial sea filled the sky and its fire-flecked edge bridged the chasm surrounding Elmar so that the people found themselves standing on its very shore. The wind died as suddenly as it had risen. Then, with Oswain at their head, those on the battlements hastened down to join the milling crowds. People and animals eagerly made way for them and there was much cheering and backslapping. Whatever else was happening they knew that their once fearsome enemies were thoroughly vanquished.

'Well done, everyone. Well done,' chortled King Argil as he passed through the crowds. 'Medals and knight-hoods all round, I think!'

Sarah and Andrew, Peter and Alena, grinned at each other.

'This is just amazing! What an adventure!' said Andrew. 'I wouldn't have missed this for anything.'

'Me neither,' agreed Peter.

'Doesn't that sea – I don't know what else to call it – look beautiful?' said Sarah. 'It's so deep and clear that it must go on for ever.'

If the citizens of Elmar had but known it, many others, including the loyal inhabitants of Traun, also found themselves standing on the edge of that crystal sea. All over the world it linked the faithful servants of Elmesh to his star.

'I just wonder what will happen next,' said Princess Alena.

Overhead, a shining canopy made up of millions of white eagles filled the sky. Suddenly, one swooped down towards Oswain and his companions, and a high-pitched shriek echoed through the air.

'Arca!' cried Sarah as soon as she saw him. 'I knew you would come.' She ran forwards with her arms outstretched in welcome, and as a result was unwittingly the first person to step onto the celestial sea.

'Hail, Sarah. Hail, O noble servants of Elmesh,' he cawed as he alighted to stand on the crystal sea. Sarah threw her arms around his neck, and the servant of Elmesh who normally showed so little of his feelings seemed at that moment to smile with delight.

'Now is the time to end all time and for Elmesh to make all things new,' he announced. 'Yet the faithful are not forgotten, nor are all partings for ever. Behold, now has come the moment for the honouring of the worthy servants of the Most High!'

The eagle raised a wing. To the utter amazement of the onlookers a vast procession began to stream from the very heart of Elrilion. As it did so, it split into many different lines that made off in various directions across the crystal sea. One line made straight towards Oswain and his companions. The skies filled with a great fanfare as they approached and everyone strained forward to see just who they were.

The first in line were forest-folk, whom Trotter recognised at once. These were the heroic animals who had died long ago during the wicked reign of Hagbane the Shadow-witch. With faltering steps the aged badger made his way, trembling, onto the crystal sea and reached out his paws to greet them. His old eyes were moist with emotion.

'Lemian, Surbut, Cauldia,' he quavered as they drew near. 'Gilda, Sigrum, Tarant! All of you!' Tears were in their eyes as they threw their arms around their faithful old leader.

Another fanfare sounded through the heavens and a nobly-dressed stoat stepped forwards.

'It's Aldred!' cried Sarah. Peter and Andrew ran to join her. Together they embraced the heroic stoat who had once sacrificed his life to save theirs.

'I see it was not wasted,' he said quietly. 'You have well honoured my small sacrifice.'

'Oh, Aldred, we are so glad we can at last say thank you to you.' Sarah wept as she spoke and her brothers added their own heartfelt thanks.

Trotter had at length finished greeting all his old friends and as they took their place with the rest of the forest-folk in Elmar, the old badger found himself standing alone and frail on the crystal sea. Anxiety lined his face and he looked very vulnerable.

Then she came.

To another great fanfare, a beautiful queen arrayed in great splendour glided towards him.

'Ah,' breathed Oswain. 'The most noble of ladies approaches.'

Trotter looked up and his eyes filled with tears. Relief flooded his face. The beautiful queen was none other than his own dear departed wife, Mrs Trotter.

Slowly, hardly believing his own eyes, he walked towards her and the years seemed to fall away from him as he did so. He reached out his arms. She stretched out hers and they were reunited at last.

'It has been too long,' he breathed. 'I've been so lonely without you.'

Mrs Trotter embraced her husband. 'Although I have been blissfully happy I have missed you too,' she replied. 'Never will we be separated again, my dear husband.'

Peter, Sarah and Andrew, hardly daring to intrude, stood awkwardly nearby. Mrs Trotter spotted them.

'Well, this is a grand meeting. Just look at me! Did you ever wonder, my dears! I can't offer you a cup of tea and cakes just yet,' said Mrs Trotter. 'But I can tell you there is better still to come.'

'Oh, Mrs Trotter!' cried Sarah, and she ran into the badger's arms.

Surin stood with Princess Alena and the King and Queen of Elmar. A single slender lady advanced. He stared at her open-mouthed and was suddenly filled with shame. For this, he recognised at once, was Tassia, his wife. Long ago he had arranged for her to be assassinated when she had fled his palace with her baby daughter, whose name was later changed to Princess Alena.

He did not move – dared not even look up as she drew near.

Her voice was mellow. 'Surin. Surin whom I loved. Little there is to say now except truly you are forgiven, for Elmesh makes all things well,' she said.

Surin knelt and kissed her hand. 'I am altogether unworthy and full of remorse. Thank you for your forgiveness,' he croaked.

Then Tassia turned to Alena. There was silence as they gazed at each other.

'Mummy?' whispered Alena. 'You are my mother? The one I never knew?'

Tassia nodded and her eyes were aglow. 'Yes, daughter. I am your mother,' she replied softly.

At once they flung themselves into each other's arms, and in those moments all was made well.

Then Tassia turned to the aged King and Queen of Elmar. 'These too are your parents, Alena, and true of heart they are indeed.' She bowed low before them. 'My Lord and Lady, I thank you from the depths of my heart for your kindness to my daughter. Nothing do I steal back of what you gave freely to her.'

'All our love is one,' acknowledged Queen Talesanna. 'We were honoured to raise her.'

'Quite so. Quite so,' agreed King Argil gruffly. He seemed to have something in his eye.

'Even though I was a pain at times,' laughed Alena

as she sniffed away the tears. Everyone laughed with her.

Surin and Tassia gazed hand in hand across the sea. Whether it was a trick of the light or otherwise, they found they could see the people of Traun. Karador had somehow been transported and now stood with Clea and his daughter Tarinda. They were greeting many of their kinsfolk.

'Your kingdom truly is safe now,' whispered Tassia to Surin.

Meetings and greetings continued. Trotter was reunited with his father, Rufus the Strong, who said he had done a good job. Heroes and martyrs, ordinary good folk who remained faithful in spite of difficulties, all were honoured in the great procession. Even the Barkums and the Glubs managed to turn up. It was the greatest day of rejoicing that anyone had ever known.

At length it was over and all the peoples had gathered upon the crystal sea. Then without anyone saying a thing, a hush fell upon the multitudes. All ears were opened.

The air filled with the deepest, richest harmony that anyone had ever heard. It was such music that it saturated people's senses and they seemed to become a part of the sound, and the sound a part of them. Golden colours flooded their hearts. All manner of joyful images bounced around their minds. Cows did cartwheels over the moon and Humpty Dumpty became a bouncing ball. Little Miss Muffet played ring a ring o' roses with the spider, Jack and Jill rolled up the hill and the fine lady rode to Banbury Cross on a kangaroo. And that was only what went through Sarah's mind.

Then everyone turned and looked out across the celestial sea.

Something very special was about to happen.

21

The King Comes

Peter was the first to notice that his feet were wet.

Until a few moments ago everyone had been standing on a smooth crystal sea of the most transparent blue. Now gentle wavelets lapped about the calves of their legs. Utterly amazed, Oswain and his entire party discovered that they were standing on what felt like the sandy bed of a shallow warm sea. They might have been at the seaside – if you allowed for the fact that this was quite unlike anything anyone had ever experienced before, what with the starlight, the music, and a million white eagles hovering overhead!

Sarah sighted dolphins.

'I thought I recognised that sound,' she cried with excitement. 'Look, there they are. Out there.'

'You're right!' exclaimed Peter, shading his eyes against the starlight.

Sure enough, they had spotted dozens, maybe hundreds, of dolphins cavorting in the water and humming in their rich cello-like voices. Dolphins like these had once carried them to safety when they were trapped on the island of Gublak the goblin, and for the first time it dawned on Peter that what he was hearing was the harmonious grace of their movement through the water

turned into sound. For those who could hear it, dolphins spoke with their bodies more than with their
mouths. 'Come on!' he cried, and the three children ran
splashing and laughing towards their aquatic friends.
Many others followed.

'We greet you, O honoured servants of Elmesh the
Most High,' sang their voices in unison. 'Fair is the day
that dawns anew to greet the coming King. Follow now
with joyful steps the paths of true delight traced
through the sea of Elmesh's love! Come, and do not fear,
for your shining hope awaits!'

So, with the myriad ranks of glittering white eagles
still hovering above them, the great company began to
wade after the dolphins. Leaping and splashing, singing
with triumphant joy, the creatures drew them ever on
towards the glorious star that filled the far horizon.

'Isn't this fantastic!' cried Andrew. He splashed Sarah
and started a water fight. Tatters barked with delight
and soon everyone was joining in the fun.

'Come on,' laughed Oswain. 'We've still got a way to
go. And you don't want to get left behind, do you?'

'No way!' declared Peter. 'I want to find out where
we're going.'

The water was warm and wonderfully blue. At first it
remained shallow, yet no one could see the bottom or
tell what it was that they walked upon. Before long, it
reached to their waists and some began to wonder if
they would have to swim for it, because the dolphins
now not far ahead obviously needed deeper water. Yet
this was no ordinary sea and however far they waded,

the waters never got deeper and nobody feared drowning. Even young children were no more submerged than their parents, and as they journeyed they laughed and played together.

How far Oswain and his companions waded no one could say, for time and space seemed strangely different and unimportant. Looking to the right and the left, they could see that the sea was filled with hundreds and thousands of people and animals of every conceivable kind. Everyone followed the call of the dolphins.

Peter wondered at the sight. It was like a mighty pilgrimage from the past into the future. His memories of where he had come from were fading fast and with a jolt he realised that the old world of Caris Meriac really had passed away for ever.

His thoughts were broken as a pelican flew into view. Its flight was shaky, and moments later it belly-flopped next to Peter with an untidy splash.

'Wheezer!' he gasped as he saw who it was. 'You've come too.'

'Well, I'll be blowed if it isn't my old friends,' the bird quavered. He gazed at the children through a pair of lopsided spectacles. 'I didn't recognise you. Do you mind if I paddle along with you? I'd feel a bit safer that way. Besides, I don't want to get tangled up with that lot up there.' He eyed the hovering eagles.

'No, you come with us,' insisted Sarah. 'We don't really know what's happening, but it's ever so exciting.'

Even as she spoke, they saw the most amazing sight. A perfect circular rainbow came into focus straight ahead of them. It hung low on the horizon just above the sea, like the rising sun, and it was to this that the dolphins were leading them. Around it was a second, paler, rainbow. Andrew noted that the colours of the outer one were reversed so that the indigo was on the inside and the red on the outside.

At the sight of the rainbow the dolphins' song rose to a great crescendo and the whole universe seemed to tremble with the glorious sound. Hearts swelled with expectancy, and with renewed energy the multitudes surged forwards. This was their destiny!

In the middle of the rainbow a pale grey shadow appeared. At first it was faint, but before their wondering eyes it grew steadily brighter. There was no doubt about it – someone was standing in the centre of the halo. Filled with awe, the people came to a standstill and marvelled at the sight.

'It is surely no less than the glory of Elmesh,' Oswain gasped in a whisper. He bowed his head in homage as the only true King was revealed, the One by whose life all worlds existed that were, that are, that ever will be.

All across that broad sea people bowed with him. Peter, Sarah and Andrew knew about royalty in their own world, but at the sight of Elmesh they discovered the meaning of real majesty. Visions of vast galaxies, towering mountain masses, thundering waterfalls and plunging canyons, sweeping plains and surging seas, tall trees gleaming gold in the setting sun – all were only a dim hint of the glorious truth now revealed to them.

No one could describe the radiant form of Elmesh. It

was beyond words and images. Transfixed with wonder, tingling with a strange mixture of fear and joy, the multitudes gazed in breathless adoration. All the hopes, all the dreams, all the pure longings and desires that any had ever felt were found fulfilled within the glorious sight. At last they knew the meaning of all the true stories. Every hint of love and loyalty, each act of courage and kindness, every true joy and delight pointed to this moment.

Some wanted to laugh, others to cry. Most managed to do both at once. There arose unbidden a mighty song whose chords soared and resounded through the heavens as unnumbered thousands – people, forest-folk, dolphins, eagles – joined in harmony. 'Elmesh is Lord of all! Elmesh is Lord of all!' they sang and it seemed that the song would go on for ever.

A vast wave of love swept across the sea. It engulfed everyone, from the smallest animal to the mightiest ruler. No one could feel more loved, and nobody felt less loved; all were equally accepted in the boundless eternal embrace of Elmesh.

Then Elmesh spoke. Peter, Sarah and Andrew heard his voice, but it did not boom across the heavens like the pretend voice of God in films. Instead, each one heard for themselves in a very personal way. It was like that for everyone.

'Welcome home, Sarah. You have dreamed and hoped, you have searched and yearned. Now you have truly found what you longed for. Be at peace. At last you are safe and free from all your fears.

'Andrew, you are full of good humour and have the gift of laughter. You have not always been understood, but no more will anyone think that you are silly because of your love of fun. Now you are free to celebrate the wonders of life and to fill people with joy.

'Peter, you have grown to be a man. It is time to stop fretting. Do not be anxious any more. You wanted to be wise but were afraid people would laugh at wisdom resting on young shoulders. Listen well; you shall be granted understanding of all my deep mysteries, and no one will despise you again.'

Then Elmesh started to laugh with a boundless, triumphant joy that shook the universe to its roots. And that joy ended all wars and violence; it bridged the chasms of pain and healed all sadness and sorrow. Fear fled for ever; death died. Broken lives were made whole and downcast eyes began to shine with hope.

'Come!' cried Elmesh. 'Let us celebrate the death of darkness and the dawn of a new world. Enter your reward.'

Filled with awe and wonder, trembling and expectant, Peter, Sarah and Andrew, along with everyone else, responded to the invitation of Elmesh. Running and splashing, laughing and shouting with glee, they streamed towards the rainbow and passed into his glory.

So the faithful peoples finally left behind their broken world with all its pains and sorrows. They crossed the celestial sea and entered into the eternal light of Elmesh's love.

* * *

'Wow! Just look at that!'

They were standing at the top of a long sloping valley that was clothed in fresh green grass. At the bottom ran a shining serpentine river and in the distance lay hazy mountains and rich forests. The air smelled sweet and the sun warmed the earth with the promise of a wonderful summer's day. All around them they could feel and sense the presence of Elmesh.

Andrew was the first away.

'Come on!' he cried. 'Race you to the river!'

Peter and Sarah chased after him. The next moment, all their friends came running too. There was Trotter and Mrs Trotter, Foxy, Aldred, Stiggle, William, Mary, Fumble, Mumble and Grumble, Flip-flop, Tatters, Hercules, Horatio and the great company of other forest-folk, all bounding and tumbling down the hillside together.

Running, dancing and leaping, delirious with delight, joy-filled hearts embraced their new life in a brand new world. Years fell away from the aged. Cripples were healed. Wheezer's spectacles fell off and he could see properly for the first time in years. 'So that's what the world looks like,' he marvelled. Firewind, with a loud neigh, raced down the valley in the company of the horses of Arandell. Such pastures awaited them as they had only dreamed about!

Argil and Talesanna, Oswain and Loriana, Surin, Tassia and Alena, Karador, Clea and Tarinda, Rolan and Suen, Danir and Haemor, Garvan, Filban, Rag, Gisana, Gumboil, Dringol, Brankleshanks and a vast host of others followed on. Friends and comrades ran side by side, and the world was filled to overflowing with the laughter and frolickings of its new inhabitants.

They quickly discovered that it was a world where you could leap over trees, or run straight through them if you wished. It made hide-and-seek a really interesting game! You could swim under water without having to hold your breath and walk as far as you wanted without ever getting tired. If you fell from a tree you could land like a cat and not hurt yourself.

There were no bullies. Everyone was friendly and nobody ever felt lonely again. Fighting and war, famine and disease were things of the past. Nobody got chickenpox or whooping cough or measles. There were no runny noses and no influenza. Food grew in abundance, and it was the most delicious that anyone had ever tasted. It was a world without sorrow and without ending.

The presence of Elmesh was everywhere. You could feel him smiling, laughing, guiding and teaching. At the beginning and end of each day, and often at different times during the day, you could sing his praises. Always and at once the great white eagles fluttered round and other people or animals appeared as if from nowhere to join in with you.

However, Elmesh did not intend that his people

should simply sit around all day. Holidays are fun, but not good if they go on for ever. He gave them fresh skills in order to plant and build, to make music and art, to invent and explore their new world. There was much to learn, though learning was always a pleasure now and nobody found it too hard.

Time had no importance in this world. Nobody counted hours and days, or weeks and months. Yet every day was different and dawned with such exciting possibilities that nobody ever got bored.

It was while they were exploring a particularly inter-esting crag of rock on one such day that Peter, Sarah and Andrew spoke together.

'Will we ever go back, do you suppose?' said Andrew.

'I don't think we can ever go back to Caris Meriac,' Peter replied. 'Oswain's old world doesn't exist any more. At least, not for us. And I'm not sure we could even get back to our own world.'

'I don't want to return anyway,' said Sarah. 'I'm so happy here. Really happy.' She pulled up her knees and sat looking thoughtfully out over the valley. 'I do won-der about Mum and Dad, though. And our friends. I hope they find the way here too, so that we can all be happy together.'

'Quite right,' said a familiar voice. 'Let us truly hope so, eh? You may yet have your heart's desire, if I'm not very much mistaken.'

'Trotter! And Mrs Trotter!' they chorused as the two badgers appeared from round the other side of the rock.

'I've brought a picnic for you, my dears,' said Mrs

Trotter with a knowing smile. 'I thought you would like a nice cup of tea and some cake. What do you think? Just like old times, only better.'

'Just like old times, only better!' they laughed.

THE END
or
THE REAL BEGINNING

For Peter, Sarah and Andrew did at length and on this occasion return to their own world, and although as is the way with such tales no time at all seemed to have passed, they somehow knew that they were not quite the same children as they were at the beginning of their adventure.

'I feel grown up all of a sudden,' said Sarah as they chatted late at night over hot chocolate. 'Like, who wants to be pathetic and bitchy anyway?'

Peter laughed. 'Well, you weren't that bad really. I suppose. Just sometimes.'

'You can talk! Anyway, you've changed too, Peter. Less worried-looking, like you're not carrying the cares of the world on your shoulders any more.'

Her brother nodded thoughtfully. The future would be OK. He would enjoy his life and shoulder the responsibilities of growing up with a lot more confidence.

As for Andrew, well he had discovered that the gift of laughter also needed the gift of love. He would never be too serious but he would grow into a very caring person and bring happiness to a lot of people.

'I think maybe we know what life is about now,' Andrew said. Then, smiling brightly over his steaming cup, he added, 'And one day, when it's right of course, we'll join Elmesh and our friends in a brand new world – and this time it really will be for ever.' He raised his cup. 'To Oswain, our friends, and the Guild of the White Eagle!' he declared.

Peter and Sarah raised their cups in ageement. 'To Oswain, our friends, and the Guild of the White Eagle!' they replied.

Oswain and the Battle for Alamore

by John Houghton

Discover the secret of Oswain's past and the awesome power of the Merestone.

Everyone loves an adventure story, but it's a bit different when you're actually part of one – as Peter, Andrew and Sarah find out when they climb into a tree and end up in the Great Forest of Alamore.

Through courage and loyalty, laughter and tears, join Prince Oswain and Trotter the badger as they struggle against the evil tyrant Hagbane in this fast-moving, action-packed story of the battle between good and evil.

'. . . as exciting and tense as Harry Potter' – Shaun Millward, aged 10.

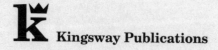

Kingsway Publications

Oswain and the Mystery of the Star Stone

(Book Two)

Powerful forces are on
the move . . . Princess Alena
has run away, wearing the
precious Star Stone. Gublak
the goblin wants the Star Stone
more than anything else in the
world.

Meanwhile, Peter, Sarah and
Andrew are having trouble
with pirates.

K **Kingsway Publications**

Oswain and the Quest for the Ice Maiden

(Book Three)

Big trouble is brewing in Kraan as Surin's army prepares for war. The chief sorcerer of the order of Thorn has offered the king his long-awaited chance to take vengeance on the South. If he succeeds Oswain and his kingdom will be destroyed. Oswain's only hope is to find the Ice Maiden before it is too late.

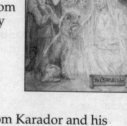

Peter and Sarah join him in a dramatic race against time. Meanwhile Andrew and his scruffy dog Tatters seek help from Karador and his band of fugitive slaves.

The fate of the free world hangs in the balance as the tiny company stands against the combined might of Surin's army and the sorcerer's schemes.

Kingsway Publications

Oswain and the Secret
of the Lost Island

(Book Four)

Peter, Sarah and Andrew find
themselves once more in
Oswain's world for the most
dramatic adventure of their
lives.

On a strange lost island,
renegade penguins are involved
in a terrible plot that will allow
an old enemy back into Caris
Meriac, and Tergan the dragon
is stirring from his slumbers.

Oswain and the Ice Maiden
join forces with the children to save the world from an
awful fate. In doing so, they will also discover the long
hidden secret of the lost Island.

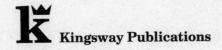 **Kingsway Publications**